Tinder

SALLY GARDNER
Drawings by DAVID ROBERTS

Tinder

Chapter One

Once in a time of war, when I was a soldier in the Imperial Army, I saw Death walking. He wore upon his skull a withered crown of white bone twisted with green hawthorn. His skeleton was shrouded with a tattered cloak of gold and in his wake stood the ghosts of my comrades newly plucked, half-lived, from life. Many I knew by name.

It was on the second day of November 1642, in the midst of the battle of Breitenfeld, when our regiment had been trapped in the great forest, caught between the criss-cross of trees and the oncoming guns of the enemy. Cannon blast sent fire into the woods and in the smoke I couldn't tell which way the fight ran. In the distance, the sound of horses, bridles and harnesses. I'd been in battle since dawn. Like my comrades, I'd fought for all I was worth, though I knew ours was a hopeless cause. About me lay the dead and the dying, their blood – our

blood – made the carpet of leaves more crimson than autumn had intended.

That was when I saw Death.

He seemed neither surprised nor impressed by the number of souls he had gathered that day. He simply asked me if I was with him.

I looked upon the ghostly army and wondered if it wouldn't be best to follow for, in truth, I'd had enough of war, had seen too much of man's inhumane heart.

'I wait for no one,' said Death.

'You've feasted well today,' I said. 'What difference would my soul make?'

It was then that Death and his ghostly army vanished. In their place a thick mist rose and through the mist a horseman came charging, sword in hand. Without another thought, I turned and ran. I ran until every muscle, every sinew strained to the edge of breaking. I ran until I had no breath left, my boots giving out before my legs fell away beneath me. I ran until the ground and I became one. I lay unable to move, only stare at the canopy of leaves all golden, all falling in spirals of colour. I listened for the sound of hooves, for the howl of a wolf, for the growl of a bear. I knew well that if the battle did not kill me then the forest would, for the smell of blood brings beasts out to feed. I lay injured, a bullet in my side, a sword wound in my shoulder, watching night creep through the trees. Maybe I should have gone with Death when he offered me his bony finger.

Chapter Two

I woke to find a fire burning and around me,
stuck into the moist earth, were poles. On
each hung an array of boots and shoes that
must have once belonged to fine ladies,
gentlemen, peasants and soldiers alike.
They danced without their owners in the
flicker of the flames. Perhaps this was a
dream, for by the fire knelt a beast.
He had the furry snout of a
great hog, the floppish ears
of a hare and a single horn
like that of an oxen. He was
dressed in a mish-mash of
doublets over which he
wore a breastplate.

I tried to crawl away, sure that I was intended for the great pot that hung over the fire. He looked at me.

Only then could I make out the fellow. His animal face was no more than a headpiece that fell, skin and fur, over his ears. Underneath, his face was white as ice, his eyes as red as flames. He had no beard upon his chin.

'Who are you?' I asked.

He took a cup of liquid from the pot and told me to drink.

'What is it?'

'I can do this with you awake or with you asleep,' said the half-beast half-man.

'Do what? Kill me?'

That made him laugh.

'Kill you?' he said. 'The bullet in your side has a mind to do that for you without my help. It needs to come out if it's not to poison you completely. As for the wound in your shoulder – too much blood has been lost. Drink.'

'Why would you want to help me?'

'Drink, Otto Hundebiss, drink.'

I did and my eyes became heavy. Before I thought to ask him how he knew my name I was engulfed in pain so overwhelming that it chased me from my body. I was aware of floating out of myself. Below me lay a young man, broken on the carpet of leaves. I could clearly see the half-beast half-man put his hand into the very flesh of him. Yet, surprising as it seemed, I felt nothing, detached as I was and at peace, unlike any peace I had ever known.

All around is a glorious light. It swirls into a tunnel at the end of which stands my family, their faces washed clean of hardship. My sister, her red skirt flying, runs towards me, whole, unbroken by the soldiers. My brother too, smiles, no sign upon his neck of where they hanged him from our apple tree. I am home and just as I'm about to run into my mother's outstretched arms, I stumble, fall, heavy as molten lead, so that once again I am earthbound.

With an explosion of agony I was back.

Next time I woke it was daylight and I had a thirst on me of which a river would be proud.

The half-beast half-man was sitting where I had last seen him. He handed me a mug of something sweet and hot.

'I want water,' I said.

'No. Drink that.'

'Will I fall asleep again?'

'Not like before. You will live. I have bandaged you, packed the wound with herbs. I have stitched your skin together at the shoulder – you will have a scar, nothing more.'

The drink slowly made my spinning head stop. The poles with the shoes were where I had last seen them. This time the half-beast half-man had before him some stones with markings.

'You are a farmer's lad,' he said.

'Yes.'

'The farm burned down.'

'Yes.'

'You had a family.'

'What is that to you?' I said.

'Nothing. Except I think you were drummed in to fight. You had an older sister and a brother.'

'Who are you?'

He did not answer but kept his eyes tight on me. And I felt obliged to tell him what had befallen my family, my people. I had not spoken of these things to any man since they had happened.

'You are right. My name is Otto Hundebiss. I was born in war, raised in war; in war I lost my family. I was fourteen when the soldiers came to our farm looking for food. They didn't speak our tongue. They took whatever they wanted. My father tried to stop them. They murdered him and my mother too. They hanged my older brother. The soldiers took my sister. She died, after they had finished with her. Our village, our farm, were burned to the ground.'

'You were not there that day, were you, Otto?'

How did he know these things?

'No,' I said. 'If I'd been there I would long be dead. I had been sent by my father to bring home a horse . . . '

I couldn't say more and I wouldn't have said that much to any man, but it felt to me as if I had seen my family again and they were at peace.

'Whose shoes are those?' I asked, for I didn't want this half-beast half-man to question me further. He already knew too much for my liking.

'They are the shoes of the dead. I collect them from villages, towns, the countryside, wherever war and plague spreads.'

'Why?'

'They have souls,' was all he said.

'How long have I lain here?' I asked.

'As long as it has taken for you to heal.'

'Hours or days?'

'Days,' he replied.

He studied the stones, his eyes aglow.

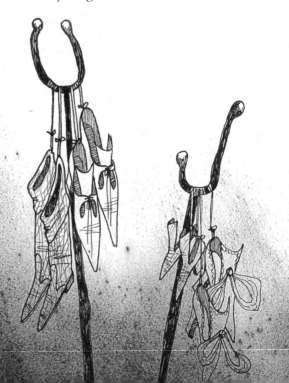

'What do they tell you?'

'That you are going on a journey.'

That I didn't find so strange for I'd decided not to go back to fight.

'I know that,' I said.

'The stones tell me that you served a captain who was a father to you. It was he who taught you how to read and write.'

'Yes, that much is true.'

'That he lost his life. Not on the battlefield, but gambling. And that he left you, in lieu of payment, five dice.'

'Did you know him?' I asked, for I could not fathom how this peculiar creature knew so much about the captain without my saying a word.

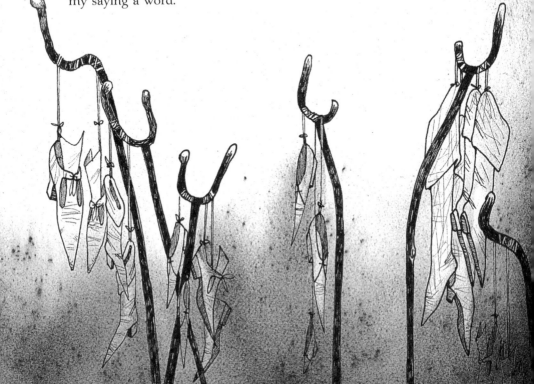

'No,' he replied. 'But I have met many such captains as the one you worked for. I have their boots upon my poles. Show me his dice.'

I took them from my satchel. The bone was stained and the dots upon them hard to read. I handed them to him.

He shook the dice in his hand and said, 'Your captain was given these dice by a pirate. They brought neither of them any luck, being the devil's own.'

I was truly stumped for he was right in every aspect. My captain had often called them that.

'Perhaps they were,' I said, 'for he lost his life cheating at liar dice.'

To my surprise he threw them on the fire. We watched them burn, the sparks rose and the dice hissed and I was convinced that I could hear in the crackle of the wood the curses of pirates and gamblers, as bone and dot became ashes.

'You seem so well-acquainted with my past. What do you know about my future?'

'When you fall in love, that is when you will come into your kingdom. Not a day before,' said the half-beast half-man.

He gathered his stones and put them away in a kid leather bag, then stood up and stamped out the fire. I could see that my questions were making him restless. I had a childish impulse to travel with him.

As if reading my thoughts, he said, 'I travel alone.'

He pulled the poles from the earth, heavy with their ripe harvest of shoes. He held them as if they were as light as a

16

bundle of sticks and no more inconvenient.

I thanked him for all that he had done, sad to see him go. We parted.

I could make neither head nor tail of what that meant. So much of what he said belonged to some alchemy of which I had no knowledge. I was about to leave when I spied the boots. A pair had been left standing near the fire. In one of the boots was a cloth bag which held five dice wrapped in parchment. These were unlike the captain's, being of ivory as white as the half-beast half-man's face, the pictures on them as red as his eyes, beautifully detailed. King, Queen, Jack, Ace, ten and nine. On the parchment the half-beast half-man had written how to use them. He said they would tell me which way to travel. For that I needed only to roll four Jacks and the fifth dice would tell me north, west, east or south. I put on the boots, not surprised to find they fitted, and rolled the dice. Four Jacks and a Queen, so I knew then I was north bound.

Chapter Three

I was raised in the lowlands. Forest was not a landscape I knew and this forest with its majestic trees, its timbered beams, its prism of leaves was a strange new world indeed. In the day I felt safe, had some sense of where I was walking. It was the dark that haunted me, for this was the time when wolves came out to quarrel with the moon. Without a fire

I knew it would be unwise to rest. I longed for a flame that would chase away the wild beasts, real or imagined.

As days passed I lost my bearings and all sense of time. Only my footsteps marched out the hours. I swear I saw my dead comrades waiting for me.

My mother used to say, 'Otto, take care of yourself.'

Stripped of family, of army, what is this self that I am supposed to take care of? In the damp darkness, all the self of me knew was danger. A creature of night terrors was shadowing my every step. I thought I saw its red eyes flicker.

Only in the dawn of a cold morning would my heart stop pounding and the sense of danger pass. In the day I rested, which left little time for hunting. I lived mainly on mushrooms and any berries I could find, but it was growing late in the year for such treats.

To take my mind off the lack of food I told myself stories remembered from the many books that my captain had stolen from the houses of burghers and such grand folk. Trophies of war, he called them. It was those books that had taught me the most, the tale of Prometheus was one of my favourites. In the hope that it might ward off hunger I told it again and again, the story of the man who had stolen fire from the heavens and brought the burning ember back to earth so that man may know the secrets of the gods. Although the more I thought about it the less I could imagine that Prometheus had ever suffered the pains of a rumbling stomach bloated by emptiness. I knew that the true fire of the soul was food.

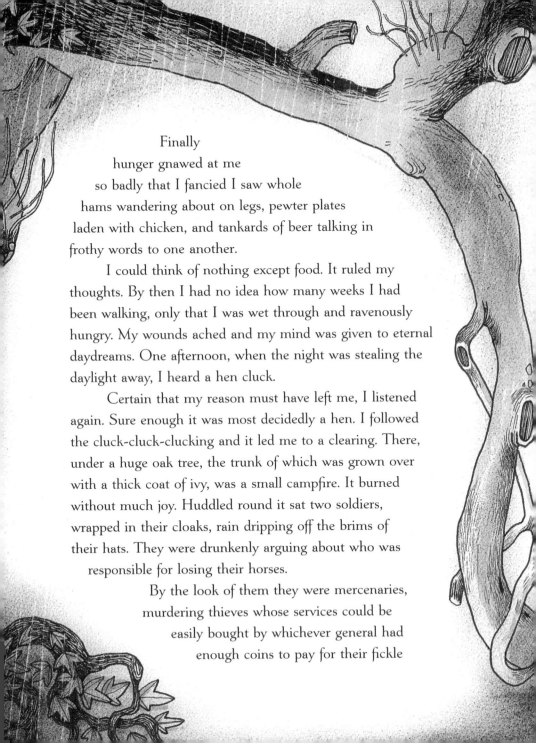

Finally
hunger gnawed at me
so badly that I fancied I saw whole
hams wandering about on legs, pewter plates
laden with chicken, and tankards of beer talking in
frothy words to one another.

I could think of nothing except food. It ruled my
thoughts. By then I had no idea how many weeks I had
been walking, only that I was wet through and ravenously
hungry. My wounds ached and my mind was given to eternal
daydreams. One afternoon, when the night was stealing the
daylight away, I heard a hen cluck.

Certain that my reason must have left me, I listened
again. Sure enough it was most decidedly a hen. I followed
the cluck-cluck-clucking and it led me to a clearing. There,
under a huge oak tree, the trunk of which was grown over
with a thick coat of ivy, was a small campfire. It burned
without much joy. Huddled round it sat two soldiers,
wrapped in their cloaks, rain dripping off the brims of
their hats. They were drunkenly arguing about who was
responsible for losing their horses.

By the look of them they were mercenaries,
murdering thieves whose services could be
easily bought by whichever general had
enough coins to pay for their fickle

favours. These two villains had been out plundering. One wore an elaborate white ruff round his neck and, from where I was hiding, the ruff made the soldier appear as if his head was served on a plate. It wasn't until his comrade looked up that I noticed he had a metal nose. It was tied on by means of a contraption of leather straps and gave him an altogether violent appearance.

In the basket next to them was wine, bread and sausage. And beside that another flagon of wine. The sight of the basket of food made my teeth water, but even through the pain of hunger I knew that it would be unwise to try to take it. In my present state I would be no match for these two hefty soldiers. I decided instead that the best plan would be to wait until the wine worked its magic and they both fell into a stupor.

Having forgotten about the horses, they took to squabbling about a maiden they'd been hunting.

In my mind's eye I saw my sister running from such big-limbed monsters as these, being caught, and being murdered. My hunger was replaced by an indigestible dish of rage.

Metal Nose's words were lined with abuse.

'You muddled bottlehead,' he said. 'We would have had the wench if you were more nimble on your feet.'

'Hold your tongue and speak better words. Didn't I find us meat and drink?' said Head-on-a-Plate.

'Tell that to the duchess, you blithering numbskull. I'm sure she will understand. If you were not so greedy we would have had the jade.'

It wasn't long before their quarrel turned into a fight, so they didn't notice the dying fire. Still neither soldier seemed concerned about the oncoming darkness, each busy at the other's throat. I was on the verge of rushing in to snatch the basket when I saw two huge eyes watching me from a little way off, glimmering yellow in the remains of the fire's glow. The moon glided over the trees and hung above the clearing and in its silver light the eyes vanished. Only the hen sensed danger. She squawked and clucked, her feathers all ruffled.

'What's that?' said Head-on-a-Plate.

'Nothing. A fox, maybe,' said Metal Nose.

'It's a wolf,' said the other. 'I told you we should have kept the fire going.'

'Brazen-headed liar! The devil take you – you never said such a thing.'

And once more they took to fighting.

Suddenly there appeared by the oak tree, as if conjured from the ground itself, a man. He was neither old nor young, no hat upon his head, his hair was thick and dog-black. He was dressed in grey with a cloak that trailed behind him. As far as I could tell he had no weapon with which to fight, only a belt that he held in one of his hands. The two soldiers, who no doubt believed better sport was to be had in the torture of this

stranger, left off their fight and
turned their grimacing faces
to greet him.

'Well, what do you
want?' said Metal Nose.

'My master,' replied
the stranger.

This sent the
soldiers off into bellicose
laughter.

'Oh, then I'm
your master,' said
Metal Nose.

I could see
that whoever this
man was there was
something fabulous
about him. He
stood proud with
no fear and not
one drop of rain
appeared to fall on
him.

By now
my fury at the
injustice of all
things had

near swallowed me whole so that I felt I would kill the devil himself to have that basket of food. I took my knife from where I'd hidden it in my boot and, caring little of the consequences, I walked into the moonlit clearing.

'What?' chuckled the soldier with the ruff. 'Are you too a scurvy knave looking for a master? If so, you've found one.'

'Do you think I'm frightened of two merry begotten, poxy drunkards?' I said.

Metal Nose took his sword from its sheath and held it before him.

'This here sword,' he said, 'has a witch's curse on it and if it so much as pricks your puny skin you will die.'

'Hot wind,' said I. 'Both full of piss and hot wind.'

The stranger stood his ground while the other soldier taunted him with his weapon. I had sobriety and pent-up wrath on my side. I fell plumb upon him, that fat-bellied pig, and being a chicken-livered coward, Metal Nose dropped his sword which I quickly retrieved.

The soldier with the ruff stood unsure whether to run the stranger through or turn his weapon on me.

'Come on,' I said. 'I'll take you or the devil will.'

Out of the corner of my eye I saw the stranger calmly put the belt he held round his waist.

It has happened to me in battle that time has slowed and every detail of a moment etched itself on my mind as if I could see for the first time, perhaps for the last time too. The man's breath was hot in the cold autumn air. I began to doubt my eyes for what I saw went against all natural science. Had I conjured this apparition? As I watched him, he became broader at the shoulders, taller, his neck thicker. His eyes were molten orbs, his teeth sharp as knives, a coal-black pelt covered his body. He was transformed into a mighty wolf.

The beast leapt at the two soldiers, who let out shrieks of terror and ran for their lives. I found myself without the use of my arms or legs, all violence in me silenced. I felt calm, my wound stopped hurting, my senses subdued by the beast's presence. The great wolf came closer. He stared at me a long, hard time and I held the gaze of those burning eyes.

'If this be my end, so be it,' I said out loud. At that the wolf turned and went where the two soldiers had fled.

I caught the hen, picked up the basket and the cloak that Metal Nose had dropped, and made my escape. A way off I heard the terrified screams of the two soldiers before the forest fell into an eerie hush.

I had in my eighteen summers seen many terrible things. Hell brought to earth on a battlefield, in the scorched skeleton bones of a city, in a farmer's yard, a family murdered, the land plundered and left to ruin. I doubted if there was enough rain in the world to cleanse this soil.

A sound carried on the ice-cold wind. A sound that, as a child, always filled me with fright. It rekindled in me stories of wolves who could be killed by bullets and werewolves who could not; how donning a belt made from the skin of a hanged man could transform you into a werewolf.

'Old wives' tales,' my mother would say, washing the blood of my nightmares away. I shuddered as I heard again the drawn-out howl of a hungry wolf.

I sat halfway up a tree, exhausted, wrapped in my cloak while the hen perched safe inside it. I'd eaten some bread and sausage and washed it down with wine. It somewhat lifted my spirits, though I was in no doubt that up a tree or not, I was still prey to the wolf. I knew well that I stood little chance of surviving many more nights like this one. I had to find shelter – a hovel, a cottage, a farm, a village. Anywhere, as long as I had a roof over my head and a fire to chase away the demons.

The rising full moon was of no comfort to me. It spread an uncanny glow while a chilly mist enveloped the forest. Above, the sky was bejewelled with stars, the heavens filled with the cries of unearthly hounds chasing their ghostly quarry across Orion's belt. The witchy moontide light made the trees look as if they had grown from mangled corpses. Twisted, devilish eyes stared at me from hollow sockets. Skeletal branches scratched at the fabric of the night and I thought that once again I'd unwittingly entered the kingdom of death. An owl hooted, foxes barked, bats screeched. But one howl had the power to silence all in that eternal forest.

When I did at last fall into a troubled slumber, I dreamed that I was with my brother.

We are walking home to our farm.
I know I have nothing to fear when he is beside me.
I began with him, we are one and all the same and
ever will be. Up ahead is our apple tree. Standing
around it are three soldiers, thrashing at the
branches with sticks, about them
a heavy rain of apples bounces on the earth.

My mother calls to me, 'Otto, take care of yourself,'

I am looking at her. Her hair is on fire, her face
blackened. I run back to tell Heinz, but I cannot
find him. Then I see him, hanging in the apple
tree, his legs twitching, eyes rolling. I try to cut him
down, screaming for help. The laughing soldiers
change into snarling dogs. One has eyes as big as
plates; the other has eyes as large as cartwheels;
the third has eyes the size of millstones.

I woke with a start to find that it was still night, bitter cold,
with only the man in the moon to watch over me.

Chapter Four

I heard a branch snap. Emerging from the
sleeping shadows, flickering in and out
of the silver beeches, came a young lad. I
noted that he was fast on his feet and carried
a rapier. I leaned forward to make sure my
eyes were not playing tricks and in doing so
dislodged the hen from its perch inside my
cloak. It fell, squawking, feather-flapping to
the ground. At the same moment the moon
disappeared behind clouds and when it returned
there was the lad at the bottom of the tree holding
the hen.

'Is this yours?' he said.

'Give it back or I'll kill you,' I said and started
to climb down the tree. 'That's my hen.'

'I, crusty fellow, have a rapier,' called the lad, 'and know well how to use it. And I don't want your hen.'

I stopped. The lad's sword was pointing at me, the hen still under his arm.

I decided to jump on him and slit his throat but was pulled up short when he said, 'What are you doing up there with a hen anyway?'

'Keeping out of the reach of wolf and bear,' I replied.

'Look,' said the lad, sheathing his rapier. 'I'm hungry and tired, and somewhat lost. I don't want to fight.'

'I've fought enough for ten lifetimes. If you can climb up here, I have some bread and wine. But any tricks and this will be your last night on earth.'

And with great agility, the hen clasped firmly under his arm, he joined me. There being room enough for two he sat next to me in the bend of the tree trunk, his hat pulled low over his head. When he did look up I was struck by his beauty, for never had I seen a face as lovely as his, eyes the colour of amber, lips rose-red and skin as pale as the full moon. Strange, I thought that nature should have given a lad such a feminine facade and such a gentle, unbroken voice. But he drank the wine and ate the sausage as well as the next man, then asked me why I had the hen.

'A trophy of war,' I said.

He laughed softly. 'Most soldiers take linen, furnishings, the virtue of young women. And you take a hen?'

'I have a cloak and a basket of food besides.'

Under his hat I could make out a smile.

'Riches indeed,' said the lad.

'What is your name?' I asked.

At that he fell silent. Ignoring my question, finally, he said, 'What army have you run from?'

'I was wounded in the battle of Breitenfeld and now I'm in the same situation as you. I'm lost.'

'You are a soldier?'

'I've been a soldier since I was fourteen. I've seen enough of war, too much, and would like to become acquainted with peace.'

The lad nodded gravely.

Flakes of snow began to fall. They sparkled like diamonds and all the unknown secrets of darkness became soft in the blue of moonshine so that the forest was transformed into a magical realm.

He put his hand out to catch the snow; a thin, white hand unused to pike or plough.

'Have you seen two soldiers?' he asked.

'One with a metal nose, the other with his head on a plate?'

'Yes,' he said.

'I took the basket from them, this cloak and the hen.'

'Do you know where they are now?'

'Both dead I would think,' I said, remembering too well the horrendous screams that I'd heard.

'Did you kill them?'

'I wish I had, but no. I think they were taken by a wolf. They talked of a young woman they were hunting. I tell you this: I'm pleased they never caught her.'

He looked up at me. 'It's not fair that girls should be bound up in skirts. I would rather be a boy, then I would be free to travel like you.' He took off his hat and threw it down. All about him cascaded fiery curls and a young woman stared at me with defiant eyes. 'A girl,' she said, 'is nothing, a pretty parcel to be given away, to be undone by a man she does not love.'

I could not think what to say but, 'My name is Otto Hundebiss.'

'Dog bite,' she said.

'Yes. That is what my family name means.'

'My name is Safire.'

'It's a beautiful name.'

I wanted to say, dazzling, like her but thought better of it, assuming she would have been told this numerous times by many suitors and would not be flattered by such an obvious comment. I was suddenly overcome with shyness and more than aware that I must resemble a wild man of the woods, for I supposed many weeks had passed since I'd considered my appearance. And here before me was a young woman I would have given much to impress for I had never seen one as bewitching.

My tongue became knotted and words felt dull with no dance in them.

'Safire,' I repeated as if her name might rekindle my power of speech, give expression to her loveliness.

Moon madness was this meeting. It had to it a dream-like quality and I felt myself drawn into some enchantment, as if we had met in between the lines of our lives and were free because of it. I had no doubt that daylight would return us to our own leaden worlds.

It never once occurred to me to ask how she came to be dressed in man's clothes or from what she was running. Such questions were shackles that tied us to this sodden earth. Instead we talked of desires, of dreams in all their wonder and bit by bit we came closer. I wrapped the cloak around her and she rested her head on my shoulder. It was as if with each cloud that hid the face of the moon a month had passed and our new-found friendship had grown until by the breaking dawn there was no question of us parting.

In the light of that stone-cold morning we climbed from the tree, our breath hard upon the winter's day. Safire picked up her hat and put it on, hiding her curls.

'Which way?' she asked.

I gave her the hen to hold while I took the dice from my satchel. I wanted to tell her about the half-beast half-man but thought better of it.

I said, 'These dice have guided me so far. I trust them to take us out of the forest.'

'I hope you are right,' she said. 'All I know is that I do not want to go back.'

'Neither do I,' I said.

'Then we are both deserters.'

I tossed the dice on the frozen ground. Four Jacks and a Queen. And so I knew we should travel north.

My captain once said that you meet people in your life who you believe will be your companions on the road, only to discover that they fall by the wayside. Others who you meet without design climb mountains with you. My captain concluded – only when the drink had made him maudlin – that it was best not to ask fate what life had in store, or where the road was bound.

'Be grateful for the journey,' he said. 'All roads have but one destination.'

I put away the dice, took back the hen and we set off, both of us lost in our own thoughts. Mine were simple enough and had to do with the finding of shelter and the making of a fire. At least, I reassured myself, I had our dinner tucked safe under my arm.

'What did the two soldiers say about the girl they were chasing?' she asked.

'It was more about what the duchess would do to them if they didn't catch her. Is it the duchess who you're running from?'

She stopped and looked at me.

Perhaps if I'd felt more certain of myself, more assured that I could be a worthy hero, I would have taken her in my arms, told her not to be afraid, that all would be well. But I didn't.

At midday fresh snow began
to fall, covering everything
in delicate lace patterns
that clung between the
blackened branches.
The bare trees held a
white veil above us.

We had walked most of the day and come across nowhere safe to shelter and as the wind blew bitter I didn't fancy being up a tree again. We were both frozen to the marrow. Our teeth chattered.

Suddenly the hen took to squawking, her feathers ruffled, frightened by something.

'What is it?' said Safire. There were snowflakes on her lashes.

Then I saw him. Through the trees, bathed in the bluish light of eventide, his long grey cloak trailing, the same man I had seen in the clearing. He stood staring at me, his eyes glowed with intensity. In his hand he carried the belt. I was as sure as day follows night that he was after us.

I shouted, 'Run, Safire, run.'

We darted in and out of the trees with the wind in our heels, we ran faster than Pegasus. We sped through snowy bracken, jig-jagging through the woods and at every turn there he was again and again, standing quite still as if he'd never stirred.

Out of breath, Safire called, 'Otto, stop! What is it you see?'

'There – there in the trees,' I said gasping, the pain in my side aching, the wound in my shoulder pounding.

'Where?' she said and looked about her.

I saw the man avoid her glance and move with unearthly speed out of the range of her vision.

'It's the voice of the trees, the silence of the snow,' she said. 'There's no one. You have a fever.'

Still I saw him watching us. The belt swung back and forth.

I heard her gasp and thought she too must at last have spied him. But no. Lying not far from us, the virgin snow turned red with blood, lay a young doe, newly slaughtered.

There was no sign of a chase. It was as if it had been placed there before we arrived.

'Stay,' I told her and taking out my knife, went nearer to the kill. A trail of blood led to an ivy curtain, clad with gobbets of snow. It hid the mouth of a cave.

Safire was by my side. I was glad that she chose not to obey me, that her will was strong, for mine felt to be melting. We stood at the entrance.

'What I would give to have a tinderbox,' she said.

She took the hen and I went into the darkness. Leathery wings flew past me into the night.

'Bats,' I said.

Stumbling forward with frozen hands outstretched, I tripped over a pile of wood.

My fingers were without feeling and the flame that I kindled at last was more valuable to us in that moment than all the gold of King Midas. We were struck dumb by the treasure trove it showed us.

Wood was stacked by the entrance. Further back was wine and bread and a pile of furs.

'A robbers' cave,' Safire said. 'What if they return? They'll murder us.'

I knew they wouldn't because I could still see him. He stood at the cave's entrance, staring in at us. The snow didn't touch him, the wind didn't move his cloak, in his hand he held the belt. This time I said nothing to Safire.

We cooked the deer meat over the fire and put the hen to roost on the pile of furs while we ate like gods in Frankenland. Never had meat tasted as good or wine as fine. The bread seemed fresh from the oven. It was a feast enough to make me forget the danger we were in, such was the warmth of the fire and the fullness of our bellies. Among the furs Safire found a quilted doublet and a red cloak. I wished it was not red.

We piled up the furs and lay down with the cloak over us. The candles were still alight, the fire well-built.

'Do you have family?' she asked.

'No. All dead. Do you?'

She turned on her side to face me.

'I had three brothers. They went off to war.'

'Are they dead?'

She did not answer but said, 'There are too many ghosts walking this earth. They weigh heavy on the living.'

'I met Death,' I told her.

She closed her eyes.

'Do you believe in werewolves?' she asked.

That pulled me up sharp.

'Why?' I said. 'Do you?'

'Yes. I come from the land of the werewolf.'

'Where's that?' I asked.

She opened her eyes and I looked into them: harbours I could rest in for all time.

'Far away,' she said. 'Tell me, what is it that you desire?'

'To take you away from here.'

'Where would you take me, stargazer?' she said.

And I told her of cities not yet built that one day we would visit, of a place by a river with high castle walls.

'And are my brothers there?' she asked.

'Yes.'

'And our children.'

My words were taken from me and I knew my heart was completely lost and, laughing, told her so. Her face became solemn, sad.

'Don't worry,' I said gently. 'It's not your concern.'

'But it is,' she protested. 'It is.'

I kissed her and she pulled away. Before I could apologise for being so forward, her lips of their own accord found mine and all words were lost to us. Kisses seemed to be a language we understood better than either of us knew.

That night my fever rose to such a degree that I was certain the man with the belt was in the cave, crouching over us. I rose to fight him and heard Safire call my name.

'Otto, Otto – there's no one here.'

My vision blurred yet still I saw him.

'Shhh. Quiet,' she said, her hand cool upon my brow. 'You're bleeding.'

I remember she said that.

A huntsman's horn, the barking of dogs roared in that bitter new day.

'I must be gone,' she said, 'before they catch me. Stay here – hide.'

I didn't understand. What could these huntsmen have to do with her?

'They will pass,' I said as she pulled away from me. 'They're out to hunt deer.'

'No. I am their prey.' She said it so simply.

All I knew in my fevered state was that I could not bear her leaving. I tried to hold her back

'Listen to me,' she said, untangling herself. 'Stay here and get well. If they see you they will kill you.'

'Who will? Who? I am not scared. I'll fight for you.'

She put her fingers on my lips.

'No, Otto. This is not your quarrel. You're too ill. Stay, please.'

'Don't go,' I pleaded.

'Hush. I will see you again,' she said. 'In my dreams.'

She stood by the mouth of the cave, the red cloak blowing.

I pulled myself up, willing my legs to stand firm. Outside a hunting party had gathered, horses snorted, bridles jangled. The dogs barked wildly as if they alone could see him, for in the middle he stood, placing the belt around his waist.

I am in battle once more. I am determined to fight
until the last breath has been trampled from me.
Horses rear, the earth shudders,
I hear the screams of full-grown men and cannot see
the cause of their injuries or where the arrows fall.
Blood. Heat. Sweat in ice. I am burning up.

Chapter Five

I woke with the hen perched on my head and found myself inside the cave, buried under the pile of furs. How I got there I did not know. The fire lay in hot ashes, the candles were burned to the wick. For one moment I had only the vaguest feeling of foreboding, then in the fitful gleam of sunlight through the ivy curtain, I remembered only too well.

My soul filled with dread when I saw the macabre hunting party of the dead. Frozen limbs stood crimson, upright in the newly fallen snow. A hand ready to grasp a bow, eyes staring, bewildered by their fate, a twisted mouth open wide in fright.

As if my last breath depended on it, I started to shovel the snow with my bare hands, wildly searching for any sign of my beloved. I thought the world had ended when I spied the edge of the red cloak she had worn. I let out a howl of pain.

Snow thudded from the trees.

'No, please,' I said out loud. 'Please, if there is a Lord above, let her not be buried here.'

Search as I might I could find no more evidence that she lay among the murdered and this gave me hope.

Wearily I went back inside the cave, snow sticking to my breeches. What now? I asked myself. I could not stay here. I determined then that whatever else I did with my life I would make it my quest to find out what had befallen Safire.

I wrapped a fur around me as I might a cloak and studied the dice as they lay in my hand. I put them to my lips and kissed them.

'Lead me to her,' I whispered. 'That is all I wish. Let me find my love again.'

I threw the dice.

They had always told me the same thing, to travel north, and I wondered if the half-beast half-man had made them roll only this way so that no one would follow him. But if that was so, would they have led me to Safire? Surely by their luck I would find her again.

Isn't that what all gamblers think? Once they win a fortune, like my captain, they believe they have luck forever on their side. I knew well that the dice are no man's friends, yet it did not stop me believing they might take me to her. They bounced on the cave floor. Four Jacks and a King. For the first time they told me to travel east. What had I to lose? I saw this as a good omen and, putting them back in my satchel, set off with the hen for company.

The deeper I went into the forest the closer together the trees became and what brightness there had been was lost. Stopping every now and then to listen, I thought the wind was playing tricks. But then I thought I heard a rasping noise, the snapping of a branch, the tread of a beast, and convinced myself that I was being followed. There it was again. A low growl. I stumbled blindly forward, felt warm breath on my neck. Whether this was real or a figment of my imagination I could not say. I only knew that it appeared closer than before, this demon that had been on my trail since I'd left the cave. I started to run, my heart racing, until I saw the sun break through the trees ahead in a shaft of smudgy light. I pushed on and came to a cart track and at last the beast – real or imagined – had gone. The god of chance was kind, for here the snow was nothing more than a light smattering. I felt like laughing, doing a jig, for a road must lead somewhere, must have a purpose.

By twilight I saw that I could travel no farther for the track was barred by tall iron gates, thickly twined with thorn ivy. I went closer and peered through. In the distance stood a castle. It was built between the trunks of three Herculean oaks. Its wooden turrets emerged from the tops of the branches and there seemed to be different floors that, higgledy-piggledy, had attached themselves to each other. Ivy covered the sides, stitching the structure together, while mosses coloured the wood itself. It looked as if the dwelling

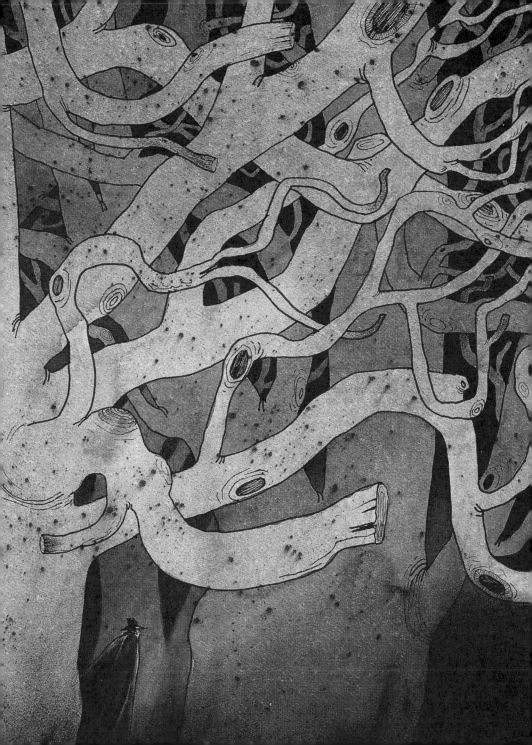

had been there thousands of years and hadn't been so much designed as taken a fancy to grow within the trees themselves. Only the windows hinted that there must have been a human hand in this feat for they were made from bottle glass that in the fading light shone burnished gold.

So much about that wooden castle struck me as strange. I wondered why it had been built so far into a forest. Stranger still that it was untouched by war. If soldiers had found it, it would have been plundered and burned to the ground. I doubted if even the iron gate would have been spared. My heart sank as a thought engulfed me: what if it was deserted? The gates were tightly locked and the path leading to the castle door ran wild with brittle, bare bushes. No smoke rose from the chimneys and there was a peculiar stillness to the place.

My mind by then had lost its moorings. I was too exhausted to make three sensible thoughts meet each other. All I could think of were Safire's kisses and the flame they had awoken in me. So it was in a daze that I rang the rusty bell-pull to see if anyone was at home. I waited and no one came. I rang it again and still no one came. Finally, though convinced it was pointless, I rang it a third time. To my amazement lights appeared in every window. I stood still, stunned at such wizardry. So wrapped was I in the wonder of the thing that I didn't notice the gates, which had been locked and overgrown, had, by some unseen hand, opened. I walked towards the castle and the closer I came to it, the farther away it appeared to be. By the time I reached the front door, night had smothered the

day. I looked at the carved images
in the wood, all of screaming heads
that seemed to shout, 'Beware, beware,'
a warning that came too late. I could
see that the gates were closed once more.
I comforted myself with the thought that
someone here might tell me where the land of
the werewolf lay.

Chapter Six

Without a sound the door opened onto a bare hall through which I came to a chamber, its walls washed white and lit with hundreds of candles. The branches of the oak trees formed a cat's cradle across the ceiling. A fire crackled in the grate of a large stone fireplace. The only furniture was a chair and a small table on which sat a bottle of wine and a glass.

I stood there, mighty baffled, not knowing what to do.

I called out, 'Is there anyone here?'

The reply was my own voice, echoing round the chamber. I thought I heard someone behind me, felt a chilly breeze brush my shoulder and spun round. Nobody was there. But if my eyes didn't deceive me, the chair had moved and the bottle, which I could have sworn was unopened, was uncorked and the glass beside it full. I was too weary to question the nature of it all. Grateful for a roof over my head, I sat and took a sip from the glass. It being of such fine quality I took another and another. The comfort of the chair, the glow of the good port wine made my eyes heavy. When I woke the chamber was in darkness, the candles snuffed out. Only the fire burned furiously as if, at that very moment, another log had been placed on it. To my surprise, the hen was seated on hay and my satchel had been hung on the back of my chair. I was not much reassured by my absent host's concern for me and my hen. There was menace in the chamber. It shivered in the air as if a trap was set and I the prey.

Through a doorway I caught a glimpse of a young woman wearing a red cloak and carrying a lantern. I called to her, knowing that she could not be Safire but at the same time hoping that by some unforeseen magic there she would be.

Clutching tight to the hen and my satchel, I followed, calling all the while for her to wait, but along the passage she went and up a narrow, winding staircase. At the very top of the turret was a small door. Only then did she turn.

I nearly lost my footing. In the flickering lamplight the face that greeted me was that of a dead girl, her eyes black, her skin fallen to bone and in her chest a huge gaping wound. In that moment the lantern went out, as did my courage. I heard buzzing and felt all about me a swarm of flies, in my ears, my hair, everywhere. The lantern's flame rekindled. The girl had gone, leaving behind a sweet, sickly smell. Now I could see thousands of blue-black flies. Wracked with fear I tried desperately to brush them away and still they came as if I was

the rotten meat they were to feast upon. My mind whirled
with the sound of insect wings. What evil was here? I fought
the black cloud with frantic energy until suddenly it appeared
to find formation, as if it had but one mind, and with purpose
flew past me out of the attic room down the wooden staircase I
had just climbed.

Shaking and near mad with terror I made sure that not
one bluebottle remained and quickly closed the door.

Slowly my senses returned. I looked about
the room and was comforted by
its ordinariness. It was
furnished with a bed
and a chair.

A window looked out through the high branches of the oak tree. I did not undress but lay on top of the covers, longing for the morning. The image of the girl would not leave me.

Up ahead is a cottage. In the afternoon light smoke from the chimney trails a kiss into the clouds. A farmer scythes wheat in his fields. The girl sits down next to me.

She wears a red cape and smells of fresh-risen bread.

'How old are you?' she asks.

'Fourteen summers,' I say. 'And you?'

'Thirteen winters,' says she.

I turn to stare at the farmer but instead I see Death reaping a harvest of soldiers, women, children.

'Is there enough soil in which to bury them all?' I ask.

'Yes,' she says. 'But many births from now men will rise from the grave of this earth, and once again wheat will grow in blood.'

I am looking into the black eyes of a dead girl.

Chapter Seven

In the light of morning I rolled the dice, clinging to those dots as a drowning man clings to a plank of wood.

According to the careful instructions of the half-beast half-man, if I rolled the ten I was to rest, gather my strength. There being only four ways to travel meant the ten was without direction. I rolled the dice three times and each time they said the same thing: four Jacks and a ten. Angrily I put them away. This time I would not heed their advice. Nothing would make me stay here. I would rather take my chance in the wilds with the wolf than remain here another hour to be tormented by apparitions and insects.

I collected my satchel and the hen and went back down the stairs, resolved to leave.

In the great chamber a servant was cleaning the grate and laying the fire. I was about to explain my presence and ask if he knew the way to the land of the werewolf when an old man with a face as wizened as tree bark appeared.

'It would be best if the hen went to the kitchen,' he said.

Whether it was the relief of knowing that there was a kitchen, that there were servants, I cannot say, but without another murmur I gave him the fowl. In return he showed me to a dining chamber.

Before me was a table laden with bread fresh from the oven, hams and cured meats, fruit of the kind only served to emperors, all the things that in my ravenous hunger I had dreamed of. Another time I would have fallen upon the feast and devoured it but now I could not, my stomach being too full of dread. It had not left me since I had first arrived at this wretched place and was made worse by the certainty that, last night, I heard from within the walls of the castle itself the howl of a wolf. Neither the sight of a snow-filled morning nor the servants had gone any way to quelling it.

I put what food I could in my satchel for I knew that once away from here my appetite would return. So intent was I upon packing provisions that I never noticed the wizened old man had returned and stood by the door watching, waiting.

'If you have finished, follow me,' he said.

Where to and why were questions he did not choose to answer.

I was left to keep up as he scurried through a labyrinth of halls and chambers, all bare, all washed white as snow. On he went, hobbleydee, up more stairs. Finally we arrived in a mighty dome-shaped place, the like of which I had never seen before.

'Wait here,' was all the wizened old man would say, and then was gone.

Wait I did. Wait for what, I did not know and as I waited I took in my surroundings. The walls rose high, the curve of the dome looked as if it was made of ice. Through it I could see the clouds pregnant with snow that appeared by some magic to flutter and vanish before one flake landed on the stone floor. I stood there colder than I had been when lost in the forest, my breath a winter's mist. Halfway up the icy walls, I spied a gallery that ran round the whole circumference of the chamber. So determined was I not to shiver, not to show fear, that I barely noticed someone had entered, just felt the frigid wind they brought with them.

Was she old? I could not say. Was she young? I knew not. She looked both if such trickery was possible. Half her face was hidden behind a black mask, her dress cut low, her hair curled, and on her neck shone jewels that would befit a queen. Her gown was silvery white, the colour of the fallen snow, and trimmed in fox. Those things I noted last, for what first caught my attention was her thumb. She had a nail grown so long that it spiralled over and over itself. She held her hand out to me, keeping her thumb separate from the rest of her fingers.

'Every traveller who comes this way has three nights of my hospitality,' she said. 'After the third night he must repay me with one favour.'

'I thank you much,' said I, 'but I won't be staying. I will be gone today.'

She came closer, bringing with her the scent of myrrh and frankincense, the perfume so strong that it fogged my power of reasoning.

She caught hold of my face, turned it towards hers.

'How old?' she asked.

'Eighteen summers.'

'Eighteen summers. A soldier and a deserter,' she said as she let go of my face and walked around me. I felt the room spinning and only she stood still.

'So watery blue be your eyes,' she said. 'So dark be your hair, so straight be your nose, so strong be your jaw. So handsome be your features.'

She held her curled thumbnail out towards me and I watched it slowly unfurl until it was as long as a knife and I knew it would be just as sharp. She placed its steely tip on my cheek.

I tried to step back, only to find myself pinned by some unseen force to the spot. I was aware of a sudden burning pain as her icy blade of a nail cut into my flesh, down over my cheek bone towards my neck.

'So red be your blood,' she said, licking the tip of her nail before it curled in upon itself again. Closer still she came until her lips touched mine. Her breath smelled of wet earth. Her eyes were lost behind the mask.

I did not return the kiss. She raised her hand and slapped me across the face.

'No one,' she hissed, 'refuses my hospitality. No one. What, soldier, do you not find me desirable?'

I kept my tongue still. For my answer would be, 'No.'

Her hand travelled down my body to my breeches.

'Ah. You have never lain with a woman,' she said.

My blush might have betrayed my answer.

'Do I not arouse you, soldier?'

Never, I thought, never.

She hissed in my ear. 'Three nights, do you hear me? Three nights and not an hour more. Then my favour I will claim.'

Chapter Eight

Next morning the castle argued itself back to life. Silent servants went about their duties as before and only the wizened old man had any words to say and none that were of any help.

No one stopped me exploring and I spent my time searching for a way of escape. It was futile. It mattered little how many chambers I found or doors I opened, none of them led to the outside world. Instead I discovered a vaulted passage lined with lanterns. Strange as it sounds, I heard two lanterns chatter to each other with tiny tongues of flame.

One said:

'A secret told is mine to tell.

'Of truth and lies, the lesser hell.'

The other:

'I hear it said she broke the spell.

'The tinderbox is buried well.'

Quickly I closed the door on them. I wanted to hear no more. I felt that my quest to find Safire was over before it had begun.

Time weighed heavy. Hours drew themselves out, each frustrating minute longer than the last, until by necessity the day condemned itself to night. It was then that all the servants vanished but the fires were kept alight by invisible hands and a meal was served in the dining hall though not one soul did I see. On the third night I lay awake, fearing the kind of favour the Lady of the Nail was going to demand of me.

I remembered with shame the times I had accompanied my captain to the whore house.

'The whores will teach you how to be a man,' he had said.

Yet for all their encouragement, I had been unmoved by their attentions.

Perhaps it was because I had seen the butchery of too many soldiers. There was no love in their actions, just drunken lust. They boasted of the women they had lain with, the whores they'd had. All were no more than cattle to them and could be slaughtered without regret, the war a poor excuse for an orgy of violence and debauchery. I had never wanted to be a part of it. If I knew nothing, I knew this: I could not lie with the Lady of the Nail. The very idea of touching her paper flesh – or worse, she touching mine – filled me with revulsion.

If I were an actor I would take on the role of my old captain who was a dog when it came to the ladies, then I

would boast like many that I could make love to anyone, young, old or indifferent, as long as she wore a skirt and had 'yes' upon her lips.

But I was no actor. I had no disguise. All I have had on the stage of life is the me that is myself. Only with Safire had I caught a glimpse of what poets meant when they wrote about love. Love takes you out of the dung heap and shows you the stars. This world without love is but an unlighted candle. I had read of passion that changed everything, of love worth dying for. I would find Safire. I would love her. I would set us free. And with that thought I fell asleep.

Through candlelit curtains I see my beloved,
beautiful beyond imagining. This is our wedding
day. In a bedroom she is undressing. Her farthingale
and petticoats lie abandoned. Now she stands in just
her chemise.
'Close your eyes,' she says.
I do, my blood on fire.
'I have come to claim my favour.'
Ice freezes all desire. I am limp, life undone flows
from me. It is the Lady of the Nail.

I woke in a cold sweat. I wondered if there was some potion I could take that would make me into a bull, then I could be free of this place. I laughed out loud at the thought. No, tomorrow I would have to service the Lady of the Nail or die. My wound hurt and I heard, as I had on the first night, the howl of a wolf. This time there were three and one so mighty that the floor moved like a rug that had been shaken.

The dreams I'd had as a child had been to do with the farm, the family. I had prayed to the Lord above with all my childish belief in the right and wrong of things: let not the battle come to our village, keep the soldiers away.

I was determined not to sleep but my eyes closed and my nightmares returned.

I am in a graveyard. My beloved sister lies on a tomb, her clothes ripped and torn from her. I take off my doublet to cover her so that no one can see her ruined nakedness. I lie beside her as I used to when I was small and she would tell me stories.
I know she is dead.
She asks me, 'Otto, why did they do this to me?'
'I don't know,' I say and I hold her frozen hand.
'I should have married,' she says. 'Had children, and my fields would have brought forth golden corn.
Why, Otto, why?'

Chapter Nine

Sweat poured from me and I could sleep no more.

It was on the last morning, with my fate fast
approaching, that I came upon a grand wooden staircase. How
I had not discovered it before mystified me, but then nothing
in that place worked within the laws of nature. The staircase
was carved with detailed scenes that depicted animals devouring
men: wolves, foxes, hunting down the hunters. Bit by bit it
gave up its grandeur in favour of the practical and turned into a
spiral stair that went higgly ever upwards.

At last I reached the long gallery that I had seen from
the domed room. Here, in varying heights and sizes, sat piles
of books. Here were glass cabinets filled with the skulls of small
birds and tiny mammals. Butterflies were pinned on velvet
and the beauty of their colours was such as I had never seen.
I wondered, not for the first time, if Death had been mocking

me all along, for ever since I'd met with him the strangest things had befallen me. I picked up a book filled with maps so glorious that I soon lost myself among its pages. One showed the world as round as a ball, a laughable notion when learned men know the world is flat. Even if you were able to walk every day of your life for more than a hundred years you still would not reach the end of it. Other books spoke of things of which I'd never heard and made me feel like an ant carrying no more than a grain of knowledge.

I would have stayed there all day and was regretting that I hadn't found this gallery earlier when I heard voices. Peering over the wooden bannisters I saw the Lady of the Nail in conversation with a woman of rank and height. Her gown was deep green, her voice a malicious whine and having no name for her, I called her Mistress Jabber.

'I want the curse removed,' said Mistress Jabber.

The Lady of the Nail laughed.

'You know of what I speak, sister,' said Mistress Jabber. 'If the prince doesn't marry my stepdaughter he and I will both die.'

'It is a piddling thing,' said my hostess. 'A simple thing to undo, if you so wish.'

'How? Tell me how.'

'Marry your stepdaughter to the prince. Then use your potions to do away with her – if you must.'

Mistress Jabber paced up and down the chamber. Where her gown went it left trails in the frost that had formed on the stone floor. Swish, swish went the hem of her green dress. Swish, swish.

The Lady of the Nail laughed again.

'Why, my dear sister, the prince has never seen her, has he?'

'It is no laughing matter,' said Mistress Jabber.

'Tell me, what does this girl look like?'

'She is fugly and loggerheaded,' said Mistress Jabber. 'Stubborn as a pig. Her hair is knotty-thick, tinged with the colour of burned oranges, her eyes are blackened wood, her skin bleached wool-white. Her lips too full for her face. As I said, she is fugly with a fiery temper that only stone walls can keep in check.'

'Now the eye of me sees it all too well, sister,' said the Lady of the Nail. 'The girl has skin silk-white, hair of fire, thick, ringlet-tight. Her eyes are evening-dark, touched with amber, her lips rose-red. Such is her beauty that you have imprisoned her. Am I right?'

I leaned forward, for surely this was Safire they were talking of. By now my hands were frozen and I had to bite hard upon my sleeve to stop my teeth from chattering.

'I advised you long ago to keep your heart locked away, not the girl. What says the duke about his daughter's fate?'

'Oh, him. He's nothing more than a wrinkle in my gown,' said Mistress Jabber.

'What tale have you woven that the duke might so

easily rest his conscience?'

'That his daughter will marry a common soldier.'

'Very good, sister, very good,' said the Lady of the Nail. 'The trouble is, this stepdaughter of yours is young, a fresh fruit from an untarnished vine, a virgin, a beauty, and you fear that if the prince should but glance at her . . .'

'He is mine,' shouted Mistress Jabber. 'Mine.'

'I have no interest in your affairs of the heart. But, sister, I do have a gift for you.'

A servant appeared carrying a plain box that he placed on a table before Mistress Jabber.

'What is this?' she asked, her face lighting up. 'The tinderbox? You have retrieved it?'

'No, sister. If I had, you, my dear, would be the first to know. It is a present,' said the Lady of the Nail.

Mistress Jabber cautiously studied the box.

'Open it,' commanded the Lady of the Nail.

'Tell me first, sister, what is in there.'

Tentatively, Mistress Jabber picked up the box. Her hand shook as she took off the lid. She rapidly closed the box again.

'Spiders,' she said in disgust. 'I hate spiders.'

'Not these, my dear. These spiders will be your salvation, should you wish to use them. Let me give you the spell.'

The Lady of the Nail went close to her and whispered words that were lost to me.

I felt my hands pulled sharply behind my back. Too late I realised I had been discovered. The wizened man held me fast

and for all my fight he never let me go. He had the unbending strength of an oak tree. I was dragged from the gallery and pushed down the stairs to the great chamber, there to await my lady's pleasure.

Chapter Ten

'This by rights should be mine,' said the Lady of the Nail. 'After all, you have been listening to words that do not belong to you.' She stood before me in her fearful beauty, her long thumbnail circling my ear. 'What did you hear?'

'Nothing but the rustle of books,' said I. 'And an infinity of things I don't understand.'

'You lie, soldier, but it is of no consequence.'

'My lady, please let me go. I am but a beggar with nothing to offer you.'

'Quiet, soldier. You found the Lady Safire in the forest, did you not? My sister told me that half her huntsmen were killed looking for her.'

'Is she alive?' I asked. 'Tell me where she is.'

She stared hard at me as if she could read all that my mind tried to keep hidden, then started to laugh.

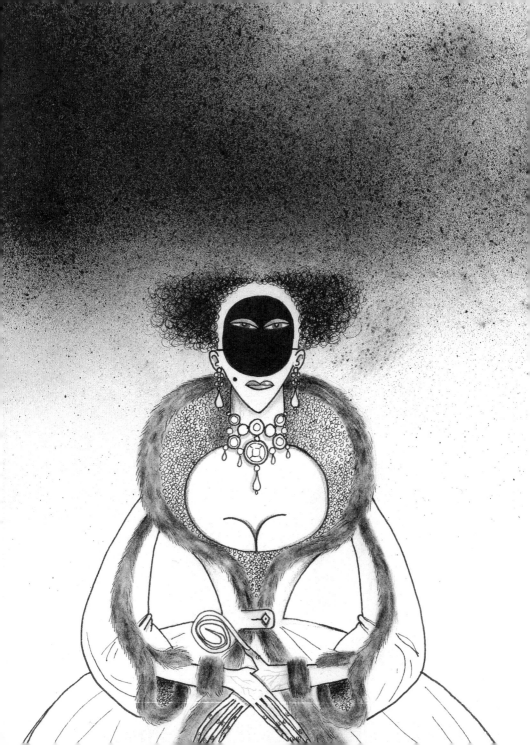

'The eye of me sees it
well. Mistress Jabber! So that is
what you call my sister. What think
you of her step-daughter? Beautiful, is she
not? She has the nature of fire with a wildness
at the root of her soul. A free spirit that not even
my sister's cruelty can crush. You know what her father,
the duke, used to call her when she was but a child? Tinder.
Tinder,' repeated the Lady of the Nail. 'She will marry the
prince. What a hellish inferno that will be.'

'I wish I had an army that could march into battle to
save her.'

'The eye of me sees it well.'

As she spoke, a swarm of bluebottles whorled from the
rafters behind her. The black masses of flies moved two chairs
towards us then rose again, smothering the light from the dome
so that the chamber became thunderous dark.

83

'Sit,' she commanded.

She leaned back in her chair and for a while studied me. I saw my grave fast approach. Then she sprang forward so that her face was close to mine.

'You wish to bed Safire, don't you?' she asked.

'I wish to love her.'

She chuckled softly to herself.

I hung my head. I knew more how to kill than how to make love. I spoke the words that were my truth. It mattered little for they would never see the light of this or any other day.

'Yes,' I said. 'To love her.'

I looked at her masked face and saw her eyes, black as a bluebottle's, shine with insect brightness.

'The eye of me sees it well,' she said. 'You fear that you will wilt before her beauty. Speak her name, virgin soldier, speak her name.'

The voice of the Lady of the Nail vibrated round the chamber.

'Not in this accursed place,' I answered.

'Speak her name or she will never be yours.'

'Safire,' I said. 'Safire.'

Chapter Eleven

The Lady of the Nail took my hand, held it firm in hers so that her nails dug into my flesh. I could have fought, refused like a squealing child, but I knew it was futile. She pulled me from my seat. There was terrible power in that grip of hers. I followed in her wake. I had no choice. I thought she would lead me to her bed chamber; instead she took me through the doors that led to the lantern-lit vaulted passage. In that muddy darkness, sprinkled with light, I heard again the hiss of candles' wicks.

'*A secret told is mine to tell.*
'*Of truth and lies, the lesser hell.*'
The Lady of the Nail pulled hard upon my hand.
'No dawdling,' she said.
I wondered how many travellers had been duped into taking shelter in this castle, only to find their graves dug, ready

and waiting.

There it was again, lurking in the folds of darkness.

'Hear that?' asked I.

'It is nothing but the whispering of lanterns,' she said. 'Do they unsettle the murky waters of your mind?'

The wicks spattered menacingly against the oncoming draught.

Here before me were mighty iron gates that rose as high as the ceiling. Through bent bars I spied a wide stone staircase leading only downwards. Earth had fallen in on it.

'Scared?' asked the Lady of the Nail, letting go of my hand.

'Only a jester wouldn't be,' I said.

On the wall beside the iron gates hung a key and a knapsack. She took them down and measured the weight of each in her hand, then said, 'This is the favour I ask of you. Bring me back my tinderbox. I left it when last I went down.'

If she had told me to fetch a necklace of stars I couldn't have been more surprised. The request was so humdrum it triggered an explosion in me. I had a mind to kill her.

'You mad old witch,' I said and drawing my knife, lunged at her, grabbed her by the hair on the back of her head and held the blade to her throat. 'A tinderbox? I could have fetched you the cursed thing and been gone from here two days ago.'

I pushed the knife deep in her flesh yet it did not yield.

'It sounds simple, doesn't it, soldier?' she said, brushing

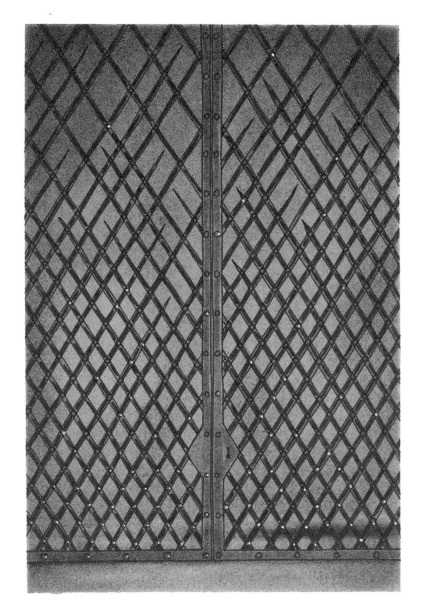

the blade aside. 'As simple as killing me, as simple as making love. But nothing ever is simple. Do this for me, my virgin soldier, and you will have your Safire.'

The smoke cleared from my mind and I saw I had no choice.

She handed me the knapsack.

I stared at it, wondering what part it played.

'Listen carefully. At the bottom of those stairs you will find three chambers. The first is filled with bronze coins. It is guarded by a beast as tall as you. Be not afraid. Release the belt from around the beast and he will take on the shape of a man. If your heart desires, you may fill your knapsack with bronze coins. The second chamber is filled with silver coins and is guarded by a beast the size of a young oak tree. Again, be not afraid. Release the belt around him and he will take on the shape of a man. If bronze is not to your liking, fill your knapsack with as much silver as you wish, but the third chamber is filled with gold coins. That room is guarded by a beast the size of a giant. Be not afraid. Once again, release the belt around him and he too will take on the shape of a man. Fill your knapsack with as much gold as you can carry – but bring me my tinderbox. That's all I ask.'

'Where is it?'

'In the third chamber, lying among the gold.'

'What trickery is this? Why would you give me so much wealth in return for something of such little value? Is this a way to make the journey to the grave more appealing?'

She smiled a smile that ivy might wear when it has sucked all the sap from a tree.

'It is enough to know, too much to see. Your freedom lies with my tinderbox. Once you have it, ring this bell here and I will let you out.'

'If I do not find it?'

'Then do not bother me further.'

She opened the iron gate.

'Wait,' I said.

The key clicked in the lock.

'All be bone and ash,' she said.

I watched her walk away, her words trailing behind her. The lanterns whispered as she glided past.

'It is enough to know . . . too much to see . . .'

And each one died in its turn.

I was left in complete darkness. The large, wide steps led to the entrance of my tomb. Blind for lack of light, I felt the stone balustrade beneath my fingers, the edge of the steps with the sole of my boots and regretted that I had ever stumbled upon this castle.

Chapter Twelve

I stood at the foot of the stone steps, my mother's words once more ringing in my head.

'Otto, take care of yourself.'

The self is me, the me is I, and that is all that's left.

By now my eyes had grown accustomed to the darkness. I was in a stone antechamber, the ceiling of earth held up on marble pillars and in between two such columns was the outline of huge wooden doors that hung half-torn from their hinges. Light spilled through their splintered planks.

The sight of the cavernous chamber, filled with hills and valleys of bronze coins, took my breath away, made my mind dizzy with possibilities. The wider world and all its revelry lay before me. The Lady of the Nail had been humble in her description. Here then was a future undreamed of. With wealth such as this I could woo Safire as would a prince, rescue her from the duchess and her huntsmen.

If, that is, I could leave the place alive.

I bent down, felt the weight of the coins as they slip-slid though my fingers. But where was the beast of which the Lady of the Nail had warned me? Look as I might, I could not find him. I had gathered a fistful of coins and was about to put them in the knapsack when I saw reflected on their dull surface the yellow eyes of a huge wolf. Dropping the coins, I spun round to see, as if materialised from bronze itself, a wolf as tall as me sitting on its haunches. He threw back his mighty head and let out a howl that sent the heaps of coins cascading to my feet. Under his paw was the severed head of a soldier, his lacy white ruff sticky with blood, an expression of astonishment pinned for all eternity upon his dead features.

Cautiously, oh so cautiously, I went closer, remembering the words of the

Lady of the Nail. Be not afraid. Release the belt and take all the coins your heart desires. Fear made me numb for I was certain that the minute I touched the wolf he would have my flesh stripped from my bones and the soldier with the ruff would have a startled companion to keep him company.

'My name is Otto Hundebiss. I mean you no harm,' I said.

The closer I went the wilder the wolf became. He snarled, showing teeth of steel. I put my trembling hand out to grab the belt, expecting to feel those teeth sink into my flesh before I could release it. I couldn't believe it when it came away. I stared at the belt, bewildered by what I had done. Then in the flicker of a flame the wolf disappeared and in his place stood the man I had seen in the forest. He wore the same long, grey cloak, his eyes dark dead, his hair dog-black. He stared blankly before him, statue-still, the soldier's head no longer under his mighty paw, but held in his gloved hand.

I wasted not one moment. I filled my breeches, my boots, the knapsack, my satchel, the inside of my doublet with as many coins as I could carry. So weighed down was I by my bounty that it was with great difficulty, wading through the bronze coins, that I made my way towards the second chamber.

These doors were not broken. They stood tall and a silver light threaded through the opening. If I had been overwhelmed by bronze then nothing could match the sight, or so I thought, of the fortune that lay beneath my feet. The chamber was larger than the one before with pillars against which were heaped mounds of silver coins that rose to the arched ceiling. Now I knew I was richer than a prince. Without a second thought I emptied all my bronze coins in favour of this treasure.

By then my head was a mirage of dreams. Drunk with untold possibilities, I lifted fistfuls and fistfuls of silver, then stopped abruptly. Where was the beast as tall as a young oak tree? Surely an animal that size would stand out among all this silver. It was then that I spied a white, snow white paw of an enormous wolf. The creature lay curled up, half-hidden behind the silver mountains. Its ice-blue eyes watched me, its jowls pulled back showing teeth the size of daggers. In this blinding dazzle of riches I could not tell where the fur of the animal began and where it fell into precious metal.

Immediately I dropped the silver coins.

Once again I said, 'My name is Otto Hundebiss. I mean you no harm.'

The wolf's growl sent a shiver of coins shimmering. In that instant I reached for its belt and it came away in my hand. In place of the wolf lay a sleeping man dressed in light grey, white hair upon his head. In his white-gloved hand he held a metal nose.

It was not hard to fathom the fate of the two soldiers I had stumbled across in the forest. They had made dainty dishes for wolves. Seeing the man sleeping there I lost not a moment. I stuffed every part of my clothing with silver. I can honestly say that here I would have been content to turn and be gone if it had not been for the tinderbox.

The third chamber looked as if no one had been that way for many years.

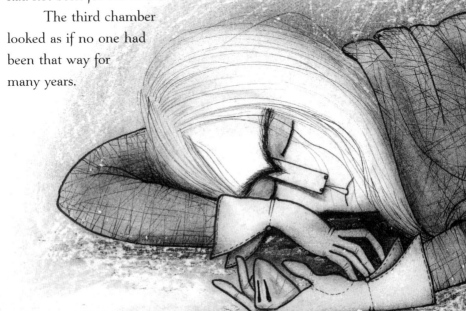

The roots of trees made a twisted screen through which fell shards of blinding golden light. It looked as if all the candles in Christendom had been lit and left there to burn.

The moment I entered the chamber my courage fell from me, fear made my heart dance in my mouth and, try as I might, I could not swallow it back down.

What sorcery, what devil, I wondered, had conjured a wolf of such monstrous proportions? His teeth alone were as sharp as pikes, as large as tombstones, his pelt as golden as the wealth he guarded.

Every part of me went to stone. The silver coins began to trickle from my doublet as if they too felt of little value among the blaze of gold.

The wolf's whole body took up the chamber and

imprisoned him so that his
head was bent towards me
and his shoulders and paws
stood like columns placed
each side of the entrance.
There was no escaping for
either of us. The belt was
tantalisingly close but my
arms and hands were made of
river reeds and seemed not to
be under my control.

Eyes closed, I hurtled
forward and pulled the belt
free. When I looked again
the room was empty apart
from gold that could buy an
empire.

That is when I saw
him, a man with golden
eyes. The same size as me,
as his brothers in the other
chambers. He stood still. His
face showed no expression.
In his hand he held out the
tinderbox.

'Master,' he said, 'what
is it that you desire?'

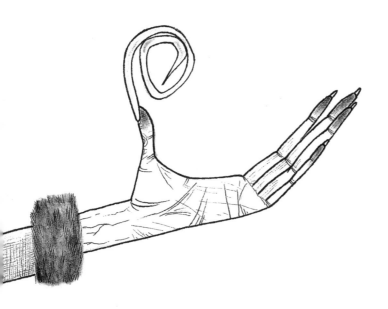

Chapter Thirteen

'I knew you wouldn't fail me, soldier,' she said, her left hand stretching through the bars of the gates, the curled nail ready to spring. 'Give it to me,' she demanded.

Her face was alight with desire.

I moved backwards down the stone step to be out of her reach.

'What, soldier? Have I not kept my word? You have a war chest worthy of an emperor. And all I ask for in return is my tinderbox.'

'Once you have opened the gate,' I said. 'Then it is yours.'

Her hand withdrew. For a moment I thought she was about to walk away, when with a sudden movement that made me jump even farther down the steps, she put the key in the lock.

I held the tinderbox tight, determined not to hand it over until I was sure of my freedom.

'Tell me why you want it,' I said.

She turned the key, though kept the gate closed.

'That is none of your business, virgin soldier. Give it to me.'

'Once I'm free,' I said, 'then it is yours.'

'Nearer,' she demanded.

Her finger reached for the tinderbox through the iron bars. I held fast. From behind me came a dull roar and the sound of splintering wood. I threw myself at the gates which, to my relief, opened.

The Lady of the Nail laughed, certain that the tinderbox was hers.

She made to snatch it but I moved it quickly out of her reach and she flew at me, her long nail screeching along the lid.

Closer it came, and closer still.

'Kill him!' she screamed. 'Kill him! Kill him!'

I shouted into the chattering lanterns, 'It's you, witch, who should be dead.'

'It's you, witch, who should be dead,' echoed the lanterns and each one of them went out.

I felt the tinderbox for the steel and struck the flint. The tinder flared. In the flicker of the flame I caught a glimpse of red eyes glowing, the quivering hands of the Lady of the Nail. The images came fast, and nothing whole to see. I felt fur brush against me and, in the dying light, saw another pair of eyes, golden, on fire with fury, jaws so large, claws so sharp . . .

'No, no, not I!' cried the Lady of the Nail.

In that second all was heat, teeth, the sound of flesh being torn from bone. Blood black as sap splattered onto the walls, seeped into the cracks of the stone.

The tinder burned out. I was shocked by the sudden silence. Then, one after another, the lanterns came alight. On the floor before me lay an unstrung puppet, its head ripped from its body, one hand upright, an island in a sea of blood, the nail still curled, so fast had the wolves devoured her.

My stomach churned and I vomited.

I never wanted to see the wretched tinderbox again, for it was the devil's box of tricks. I threw it hard on the stone floor and it broke apart.

I did not run. I could not run, weighed down as I was by my satchel and the knapsack. More I stumbled from that place, aware only of the earth trembling, the stone walls pulsating. In my mind's eye I could see the giant wolf himself rocking the foundations of the castle as if it were a child's building of sticks. At the great hall I was greeted by an orchestra of creaking timbers, the soil itself calling the wooden castle back to its roots. The hall hummed with the buzz of bluebottles. I pushed open the grand doors that led to the world outside and, followed by the sticky black fabric of whirring wings, I found myself in the biting cold.

I kept moving. My mind, dancing with the impossibility of all that had happened, was eased by the beat of one foot on the ground followed by the other. Only when I reached the bend in the track did I stop and look round. I stared in awe at the sight before me. The castle of wood had begun to fall. Its timbers tumbled down and with each beam that hit the earth a spark of fire ignited, out of which a sapling grew, until what remained was the ruins of a building surrounded by young trees, the sky turned to night by clouds of bluebottles.

Chapter Fourteen

What forest was this? Having found its witches and wolves I expected at any moment to be halted by its devils and demons. I soon sank into snow that made mockery of my journey. I cursed the lack of a cloak. I cursed my wound that began to throb. I cursed the weight of the knapsack that cut into my shoulders, now sure it contained nothing more than rocks to fool dreamers by. All the while the sun showed little inclination to make an appearance; rather it handed over the sky to darkening clouds. My mind was flooded with images of the Lady of the Nail.

It must have been mid-afternoon when I came to where the trees stopped and the earth folded on itself. My body was wrecked. By the edge of a ravine I stopped.

Here I felt safe enough to see what was in the knapsack. At first I thought my eyes deceived me, for at the top sat the tinderbox. Hadn't I thrown it down? Hadn't I seen it smash on the stone floor? Perhaps my memory was not to be trusted. But there it was, that cursed thing.

I threw it into the ravine, where it shattered against the rocks.

There could be no doubt about the gold. It went to the very bottom of the bag and the sight of it made my knees weak. Falling to the ground, I burst out laughing. I was richer than a whole marauding army. What now?

In my satchel among even more gold I found the dice. It was they that answered the question. An Ace and four Jacks. I was to travel south.

I picked up my bags and set off again. I told myself the pain in my shoulder was well worth it. If I could find a town or village before I froze to death I would be the richest man there. Thoughts of Safire took my mind off my aches and pains.

I came to a crossroads and was wondering which way to turn when a caravan came plodding into view, pulled by what appeared to be a phantom horse, so covered was the animal in snow. The driver too was a ghostly vision, with hollow eyes that shone in the flare of his pipe. Here, I thought, comes the world on wheels and it matters not one jot if the coachman be the devil himself as long as he has a cart to carry me away from this place.

'Sir, may I ride with you?' I called.

'I cannot stop,' cried the driver. 'If I do, old Nan will never move again. But if you can catch us you are welcome.'

It took the last of my
strength to jump onto the back
step of the caravan where the pots
and pans rang as loudly as church bells. I clambered up, pulled
the canvas aside and tumbled into the musty darkness, my
head brushing against tiny cloth shoes and small hands. I lay
on the wooden floor for a moment, taking in my surroundings.
Above me hung rows of dancing, raggedy puppets. Their
gargoyle faces grinned benevolently down on me, their eyes
twinkled in the gloom, their wooden teeth chattered. Careful

not to touch this company of clapper dudgeons, I joined the driver.

'Not the kind of day to be out in the forest,' said he. 'Where are you travelling?'

'Wherever you're going. It's all one to me,' I said.

'To the next town then. What's your name?' he asked.

'Otto Hundebiss. And yours?'

'I am a poet and a Gentleman of Ragged Order.'

'Are those your puppets, sir?'

'Yes. For my sins I perform mystery plays.'

He handed me a full bottle of schnapps. The warmth of the liquid set a pleasing fire in my throat. We fell into a companionable silence, soothed by the rhythm of the horse as it plodded cautiously along the icy roads, the snow blue in the twilight, the forest behind us, its shades still clinging to me. Windy words vexed my ears.

'Master,' they seemed to say, 'what is it that you desire?'

What was my desire?

To find the girl with fiery red hair, to love the girl with fiery red hair. To win her heart.

We came to a huge boulder. The light had all but gone so that in the gloom it looked as if we were passing under the snowy skirt of a giantess.

'Mistress Fortune takes good care of us,' said the Gentleman of Ragged Order. 'Any later than this and the road would be impassable.'

His words echoed as we went through the stone tunnel.

On the other side the moon hung low in the sky and in the distance was the soft outline of hills that surrounded a valley. A river ran through it, and down the winding road before us I could see, sitting on its banks, the fortified walls of a town. Beyond, spires, turrets and towers were silhouetted against the indigo of the oncoming night.

'Where are we?' I asked, hardly able to contain my excitement, for here was safety.

The Gentleman of Ragged Order's answer was lost in the canter of horses and, turning, I saw coming up behind us a grand hunting party. On one fine horse sat a nobleman wrapped in furs, his face set hard against the cold. All of him spoke of wealth. His servants came to us and demanded that we move aside.

My companion doffed his cap and pulled Nan to a reluctant halt. We had a perfect view of the passing procession. Towards the rear came a riderless horse led by one of the soldiers. Over it lay a bloodied sack. An arm and a mangled leg swung from it.

'Did you see?' I asked. 'Did see you what was on the horse?'

The Gentleman of Ragged Order chose to take no notice of my question and busied himself persuading our humble nag to move.

'Who was that nobleman?'

He shrugged.

'Who rules these lands?' I asked.

'All you see and more
belongs to the duke.'

'Does the duke have a daughter?'

'He had a daughter, and three sons.'

'Had? Are they all dead?'

'The duke's sons went to do
their father's business in Cologne and
never returned. Or so it is said. What
happened to them is not known.'

'And his daughter?'

'As good as dead.'

'What does that mean?'

'No one in the town has seen the Lady Safire
for five long years.'

Silently I rejoiced, for the dice hadn't let me
down. This was the land of the werewolf which
Safire had spoken of. I was near my love and with
enough gold to be a worthy suitor.

Lifting his clay pipe the Gentleman of
Ragged Order pointed to a hill not far from the
town, on which sat a castle. 'That is where she is
kept locked away.'

'Why?' I asked.

'There are many rumours as to why. Some
say she is touched by madness, others that she is
a witch. The truth is more twisted. When the
girl's mother died and the duke remarried, the

114

new duchess's astrologer supposedly saw in the stars that the duke's daughter would marry a common soldier.'

'And for that she is locked away?'

'You do not know the people of these parts and therefore you cannot judge their customs or their ways,' said the Gentleman of Ragged Order. 'Ask no more questions and be grateful that you have found shelter in this town. You wanted to be out of the forest, did you not?'

I nodded.

'Then that's where you are.'

The old horse speeded up, sensing stable and hay.

The Gentleman of Ragged Order said, 'Best you keep quiet if we are stopped by the night watchman. Strangers are not welcome here. If I'm asked, I'll say you are a friend of mine.'

The town's bells warned of night's approach as at last we came to a covered bridge that crossed the frozen river. There was no question of entering silently for old Nan's hooves sounded like war drums on the wooden slats. The town gates were guarded on either side by stone statues in the shape of wolves.

115

We were the last to enter the town that night. No questions were asked and the gate was barred behind us.

I had imagined that once inside the town walls the place would be busy. Instead it was dark, every door shut, not a candle to be seen peeping from any window, no drunkard reeling. Not even a mouse scurrying away, for the town was like a bed and everyone in it was soundly asleep.

'Where is everybody?'

'Nobody here dares stir after dark.'

'What are they afraid of? Mercenaries?'

'Heavens, not now. The war hasn't touched this place. Not in five years. No, the cause of their fear would keep any army at bay.'

'I don't understand,' I said.

But I knew that I did.

Chapter Fifteen

There was an inn and several taverns. I decided that as I could afford the best the town had to offer, then the best was what I would have.

The Gentleman of Ragged Order led me to the inn.

'If you want to be parted from your money then The Black Eagle is the place to stay.'

I offered him a gold coin for his kindness. He took it without a word. I had to ring the bell and knock hard on the door before it was opened by a man with a spit-roasted face and a throat full of foul words.

'I've been told yours is the best place in which to stay,' I said.

'By whom?' he asked.

'By the Gentleman of Ragged Order.'

The innkeeper mumbled under his breath, cursing the

man and calling us both vagabonds. In truth, I cared naught what he thought, though I could see he was determined to make a long harvest out of little corn.

He was about to shut the door and I quickly put my foot there to stop him.

'We do not like strangers,' he said, eyeing my tattered clothes up and down.

'I don't like being a stranger,' I replied.

I handed him one gold coin. He studied it and hummed and hawed before hitting on a plan, for he had reckoned on this being all the wealth I possessed.

'We have no rooms. Apart, that is, from the best chambers,' he said grandly and laughed. 'Unfortunately they are not for the likes of those in the ragamuffin regiment.'

I took from my satchel the purse that I had filled with a few gold coins and showed it to him. His eyes, already given to bulging, looked on the verge of falling out altogether. The door opened with ease and at last I was welcomed inside, the innkeeper calling all the while for his wife.

'How long would you be staying, sir?' he said.

'I don't rightly know,' I said. 'For as long as my fancy takes me.'

He sucked on what was left of his charred teeth and his voice changed completely.

'Sir, you should have said straight away that you were

a young gallant on the road in disguise. Very wise, if I may say so.' Here he bent towards me as if I had told him my beginning and my end. 'Your secret is safe with me.'

What the spit-roasted fool was on about I had no idea. And did not much care, as long as I was given a chamber. I remembered that my captain often said, 'Money changes everything.' It even made a floth-mouthed, fiery-faced innkeeper into a sweet-tongued charmer, though this was the first time I had seen such a thing in practice, for my captain never had two coins to rub together.

'This way,' said the innkeeper, taking a candle and leading me up the stairs with many apologies for the unevenness of the floorboards and how I should mind my step. In fact he had not once left off his cheerful chatter since he had found his new voice. The chambers were indeed large if not a little dusty due to neglect and a lack of housewifery.

The innkeeper's wife, a lumpish woman, appeared in a flurry. My arrival somewhat took the straw out of her mattress of flesh. She was followed by a flat girl, buried under a pile of linen. When the girl put it down I thought she might have had a collision with a wall, so squashed were her features. I stood by the window and watched as husband and wife started to pick at the fluff of each other's failings.

'You should have known he was arriving this evening,' she bickered.

'How could I?'

'I told you. I had a feeling in my waters.'

'If I turned over every room because of your waters I would be flooded by bad decisions.'

Their mutual dislike amused me. All the while it was the maid who did most of the work. Every now and then the wife, losing the argument with her husband, would give the girl a good clip behind the ear.

The show being over and the chamber to their satisfaction, the three of them departed with many wishes for a good rest and a hope that the devil wouldn't disturb me much. I undressed, laughing as silver and bronze coins spilled from my doublet and out of my boots. Hastily I stuffed them in my satchel, then, taking the heavy knapsack, made sure the straps were secure and hid it under the bed.

I ate the food and drank the wine that had been brought for me before sinking into sweet-smelling sheets. As the fire crackled in the grate, I felt my whole body relax into the luxury of good living.

'This,' I said to the candle flame as I snuffed it out, 'this is just the beginning.'

I am on a foray to plunder what, by right of war,
is mine to take. The streets are deserted and the
baked bodies of men, women and children lie
scattered among burning buildings.
I see my mother and father. They too are on fire
but they seem unconcerned by the halo of flames
engulfing them. They walk hand in hand.
My father asks me, 'Have you a tinderbox, son?
We need to light a fire.'

Chapter Sixteen

My chamber looked over the market square. I stood with the shutters open and watched the stall-holders put out their wares, the young girls with their clean white aprons and hair all neat. The smell of roasted chestnuts and sweet gingerbread warmed the bitter air. I was comforted greatly by the noise and the hustle and bustle of the market. I could almost believe that here there wasn't a war, so ordered did the world look that morning.

In the distance I could just see the spires of the castle rising above the town and the very idea that I was so close to Safire made me itchy with impatience. Without a thought to my appearance I had dressed and was about to leave when I heard something clatter to the floor. I looked around the chamber. Nothing, as far as I could see, was out of place. The clatter was followed by the noise of an object being dragged across bare boards. It appeared to be coming from under the bed. A rat, I said to myself and bent to check the knapsack. I sprang back the second I saw the thing, my heart near stopped in fright. There it was, the tinderbox.

The sight of it brought with it a flash of memory that jarred me and as clear as I saw the chair, the window, the bed and fire, I saw the Lady of the Nail,  her ragged body and her head in a sea of blood. Sweat poured down my face and for the first time I wondered if it was I who had unwittingly murdered the Lady of the Nail. I, the savage, blaming wolves. I'd heard of men returning from battle who had slaughtered their wives while they slept, not meaning to, not knowing what they were doing, and swearing afterwards they had no memory of the deed.

I tried desperately to find some logical explanation of its unwanted appearance. Hadn't I seen the tinderbox smashed in the ravine? Perhaps I'd dreamed it. Nevertheless, the sooner I rid myself of it the better. With a trembling hand, I picked up the tinderbox, half expecting it to bite, and threw the witch's curse on the fire. It landed with a satisfying thud, dislodging the logs, and in no time at all was gobbled up in the flames that leapt up the chimney.

Breathe, I told myself, breathe. My spirit became calmer as I watched the tinderbox burn until there seemed to be nothing left of it but cinders. I put the poker into the fire to make doubly sure that the wretched thing was indeed ashes. Seeing no sign of it, I told myself the nightmare was over. I called for the innkeeper.

He came panting and out of breath, tying the strings of his apron about him. I told him I would like breakfast and then I was going out.

'Like that, sir?' he asked.

He cleared his throat of phlegm and said that he had taken the liberty of sending the servant girl, Marie, to fetch a gold merchant.

'A gold merchant?'

'Yes, sir. I thought you might want some of the gold transferred to a more humble coinage that would not blind the merchants of this town.'

It seemed sensible enough.

'I have also sent for a tailor and a barber,' he added.

I would have said they weren't needed until I caught a glimpse of my reflection in the window. Staring back at me was some wild animal with long unruly hair and a beard. The innkeeper had a fair point. If I wanted to make a good impression on the duke when I asked for Safire's hand I should at least be dressed as a nobleman. Defeated by my appearance and the innkeeper's determination, I decided to take his advice.

His good wife brought a jug of beer and a dish of ham. Alone in my chamber, I ate. I had closed my eyes and drifted into a reverie about Safire when I felt it. Breath, ice-cold on my neck.

'Master, what is it that you desire?' whispered a voice.

I grabbed my knife and turning wildly, thought I caught sight of yellow eyes.

'Who's there?' I shouted so loudly that the innkeeper's wife came running.

I assured her all was well, and leaned with my back against the door as her heavy tread faded away.

Then, as might a child, I looked behind the drapes to persuade myself it was a daydream. I even looked under the bed again, pulled out my knapsack and carefully opened it, half-expecting to see the tinderbox sitting there. The relief of only finding gold could hardly be measured. I took two good handfuls of coins and stacked them on the table before returning the knapsack to its hiding place.

The gold merchant reminded me of a ferret I once had when I was about nine. He had the same small piercing eyes and a nose that twitched. He wore a moth's meal of a cloak, singed by sitting too close to too many mean fires. He introduced himself as Master Albert Krempel.

I watched him. He sniffed the air then moved by instinct towards his prey. His small eyes lit with lust when he saw the gold upon the table.

'What will you give me for this?' I asked.

He brought out a glass which he held up to his right eye. The effect was to make it menacingly large. After much twitching and turning of coins he wrote a figure on a piece of paper.

The sum seemed a fortune, an amount almost impossible to spend, and without bartering, or even asking how Master Krempel had arrived at that figure, the business was done. In a conjuror's trick my gold coins vanished.

Next to arrive was the tailor. He brought with him two apprentices and between them they carried a huge trunk. When the trunk was opened it contained an extraordinary array of doublets and hose. I saw myself dressed as a cavalier, the finery disguising the humble soldier. The tailor, with great pride, told me these all could be quickly altered to fit me and then he would make my best suit himself.

I was completely bedazzled by the clothes so that in no time I had become a fool of fashion, the chamber a snowstorm of fabrics. Tailor and apprentices flew hither and thither as I ordered more clothes than I had ever owned in my life.

Next came the barber, who flattered me on my head of thick hair, told me curls were being worn at court this season and presented me with a whole range of hairstyles. A Dutch cut or French? Did the esteemed gentleman want to look stern of countenance, pleasant or demure? More money left my hands as the barber, his bowls and his cut-throat razor departed.

The shoemaker arrived shortly after to measure my feet.

He had already talked to the tailor, who had appointed himself master of my wardrobe.

I thought that must be all, but I was wrong. The haberdasher had been sent as a matter of urgency: shirts, fine stockings, cambric ruffs, hats with feathers that no bird would wear. Was there no end to such fripperies? At last they were agreed upon and with much bowing the haberdasher left.

I was about to sit down to recover my wits when I caught sight of it on the table, as good as if flame had never touched it. Surely I had burned it? How then, I would like to know, by all the legions of devils, was the tinderbox there before me?

Chapter Seventeen

This was the devil's plaything. Three times I had tried to rid myself of the tinderbox, three times it had returned, trailing the grave in its wake.

Damn it. I would have said that fortune had smiled kindly on me. How many men win such a treasure trove? All that weighed me down was the wretched tinderbox. I buried it

under a loose floorboard. If
I told myself, it was out of
that a sliver of freezing
the spot.

I couldn't wait in that
let alone a whole day until
ready. I was determined to
seeing Safire. Surely that
intended for, to release her

I couldn't be rid of it, at least,
sight. I was alarmed to find
air seemed to hang over

chamber another moment,
my new clothes were
be gone, to find a way of
was what my fortune was
from the duchess's prison?

I put my satchel across
me, wrapped my muffler round
my neck and, pulling my hat
down over my face, closed my door
and took the stairs two at a time.
The houses in the market
square were made of timber, their
facades ornamented with elaborate
sculptures. Underneath, pillared walkways
offered the market stalls some protection from the
worst of the elements. Here were butchers, bakers,
sellers of gingerbread, vegetables and candles, goods
that had been brought in from the surrounding
farms. A motley feast indeed. Pedlars sold trinkets
to keep werewolves away. One was doing a fair trade

in pamphlets reporting
the latest news, all of it
to do with werewolf trials
and showing an engraving of
said beast. The supposed animal
resembled nothing of the three
werewolves I had encountered. It was
drawn like a dog with eyes as large as
plates.

    I bought a pamphlet entitled The Prophecy
and read it with interest. Safire's mother had been
the daughter of a hermit, it said. She and her father
had lived hidden in the forest and one night he had
encountered a witch who had changed him into a
werewolf. After that he was never seen again. His

The Prophecy.

·1642·

daughter ran wild, half-naked, about the woods until the duke, out hunting, saw her and brought her back to be his bride. The night she died, the night Safire was born, the forest rang with a thousand howls of a thousand wolves. The pamphlet ended saying that we all know what is written in the stars and the prophecy they tell us. That is why the Lady Safire must never be released.

I bought three more such pamphlets and, none the wiser for their gibberish, I set off in the direction of the castle spires.

Beyond the market square the houses were given to leaning towards one another, so close that they appeared joined in gossipy conversation, hanging on each other's words. What light there was hardly penetrated the alleyways. They widened out again before coming to the river and the castle walls which rose into a pinkish, snow-filled sky.

The main gates were well-guarded and looked as if they planned to stay tight shut. I had walked part way round the castle when, by a side door in the wall, I saw a group of labourers huddled against the cold.

'Good day,' I said.

The rag-tag bunch of men turned to stare at me.

'Any work going?' I asked, a plan forming in my mind.

'Be off,' said a crusty man. 'Strangers aren't welcome here.'

'I'm no different from you – hungry and in need of a coin.'

'The devil and the hangman take you.'

I stood a little way from them.

'Leave him,' said a meagre man. 'He won't last long, not in these parts. The werewolves will sniff him out and tear him to pieces, just as they did to that band of mercenaries that took a fancy to plundering the town.'

'Have you seen these werewolves?' I asked.

'Look, soldier boy. We made it clear – you're not welcome and any work going is ours, not yours.'

I thought for a moment that I was in for a fight, for they looked a rough bunch in need of exercise to warm them up. Then the side door opened and a steward came out accompanied by a guard. The labourers sank back as they formed themselves into a line of woebegone soldiers, chests stuck out ready for action. Standing a little apart from them, I did the same, mimicking their every move. I was by far the youngest man there.

'You, you, you and you,' said the steward, pointing at me and three others.

'That's not fair,' said one of the men. 'He's not from this town.'

'Scumbag,' hissed another at me.

The steward took no notice.

'Off with the rest of you,' he shouted. 'No one else is needed today.'

None of the men moved until the guard went at them and they dispersed towards the river, along the road I had just come.

The four of us were taken through the door into a courtyard.

As I tried to commit to memory all I saw there, I didn't notice the steward's stick until it poked me in the ribs.

'Are you asleep? Didn't you hear what I said? You're to go to the gardens.'

I watched with envy as the three labourers were led to the warmth of the castle. If I was inside with them, I stood a small chance of seeing Safire.

'This way,' said the steward, leading me through a gate.

I had only read about gardens such as this in books. It was laid out in the formal Italian manner, a thing of stilted beauty, planted in geometric patterns, nature brought under control by the power of man. The steward walked with me down a snowy gravel path until we reached a maze of clipped hedges taller than me. An elderly man with a ladder and baskets of white roses waited at the entrance. The steward turned and walked away.

'Pick up the baskets,' said the gardener. 'And follow the ribbon if you ever want to find your way out again.'

Our job, so he told me, was to cover the bare branches of a tree in the middle of the maze with the roses.

From the top of the ladder it didn't take me long to solve the puzzle of the thing. It was square in shape and round at the centre where the tree grew. Many of the paths led to dead ends and others tricked you into being completely lost.

By the beginning of the afternoon, flurries of snow had

136

started to fall and my work seemed as pointless as sieving salt
from the sea. Then I heard women's voices.

'Come down, quickly,' said the gardener. 'We must be
gone. We're not meant to be seen.'

He held the ribbon in his hand as if he was about to
pull us into harbour. I had no intention of climbing down but
continued tying the last of the white roses to the branches.

'Come down,' hissed the furious gardener again, shaking
the ladder. Seeing I wasn't going to budge, he followed the
ribbon, reeling it in as he scurried off.

I was pleased I had been so diligent in my work for the
white roses gave me perfect cover. I could see quite clearly
the whole of the maze below me. To the right entered the
nobleman I'd seen leading the hunting party on the road to the
town. He was dressed in a leather doublet and a fur-lined cloak.
His whole appearance spoke of money and meanness at the
same time. He was looking for someone.

I nearly lost my balance when I saw her. I thought my
longing for Safire might have brought forth a phantom. I
closed my eyes and opened them again in order to see her more
clearly. She was walking with her chaperone.

The older woman said, 'Calm yourself, Tinder. What use
is your rage? My sweet, meet the prince, that is all. It is he who
will bring you freedom from the duchess.'

'Freedom? To marry that bully would be to change one
dungeon for another.'

The prince heard this too and, making his way towards

them, trapped Safire and her chaperone in a dead end with no means of escape.

'Leave, Mistress Presen,' ordered the prince. 'I wish to speak to Lady Safire alone.'

The chaperone squeezed past the prince and I could see it cost her to leave her charge like this.

'Come back,' Safire called after her. 'Don't leave me here with him.'

The prince waited until the chaperone had gone then said, 'Come, what is there to be frightened of? I will be your husband soon. Why the modesty?'

He went to Safire and undid her cloak.

'You have the palest skin and breasts round like apples.'

'Don't touch me,' said Safire, wrapping her cloak around her.

'I have a rooster looking for a nest, my lady.'

'I hear it already crows in my stepmother's chamber.'

I felt for my knife. I would kill him if he laid a hand on her.

'Whether you like it or not, my lady, when we are married I will assail you so fiercely that you will dare not resist. What do you think to that?'

'I do not like you, nor your manners, sir.'

He laughed. A cruel laugh, such as I had heard often in commanding officers. It had the rattle of death about it.

'Manners? What do you know of manners? You who ran wild with your brothers, dressed as a boy to do boyish things.'

He moved closer to her, his breath steaming in the frigid air. 'Kiss me.'

'No,' said Safire. 'Not now, not ever.'

My grip tightened on my knife. I was ready to kill him and swing in the hangman's noose for it when I heard him shout in pain.

'You dare bite me, you she-wolf?'

At the same moment, I saw Safire running along the hedged paths. I climbed down the tree. I was so near to her, it was just a matter of taking one right turn. I zigged and zagged then heard the rustle of skirts and turning, saw her emerge from one path and disappear down another. I followed, lost sight of her for a moment and must have taken a wrong turn for I collided with her chaperone.

'Have you seen the Lady Safire?' she asked. 'Can you help me find her?'

I led her back to the tree that I had spent the day covering with white roses and climbed the ladder. Safire was nowhere to be seen and for a moment neither was the prince. The thought that she had unwittingly run into him made my blood boil and my vision a red mist of rage. A sort of relief washed over me when I spotted him. He was well and truly lost.

'Here – you,' he shouted at me. 'Come and lead me out.'

I took no notice for now I could see Safire running from the maze, her petticoats flying. I had been so close to her and yet unable to reach her to tell her that I loved her; that I, Otto

Hundebiss was now a rich man and could take her to that city not yet built.

I climbed down.

'Well?' asked Mistress Presen.

'She is making her way back to the castle.'

Mistress Presen sighed. 'Do you know the way out of here?'

'Yes, I believe I do,' I said.

We left the prince shouting for Safire. 'Where are you, my lady? You will come to heel.'

'That I doubt very much,' said her chaperone.

Chapter Eighteen

I am walking up a woody lane behind my father.
Try as I might I cannot catch up with him. Every
step he takes he grows taller and mightier. How will
I be able to ask him the question when his ears are so
far from the ground? He stops and turns towards me.
'Father,' I say, 'which village am I to collect the
horse from?'
He tilts his head to the sun and branches grow
from his hair, his arms, his hands while the rest of
him turns into the twisted trunk of a great oak.
Its leaves fall all around me, each a printed page,
a fluttering of knowledge.
There in the dappled sunshine of a thousand books
is my captain. A roguish smile flickers across his lips.
He says, 'It is your turn to roll the dice, son.'

I heard them rattle in his hand and woke with a start. The sound was coming from under the floorboards. Was the tinderbox trying to escape its tomb? I listened, horrified, as the light from the fire threw ghostly shadows on the walls of the chamber.

I tried to think only of yesterday when I'd seen Safire, of her courage, her refusal to be defeated, to be undone by that lickspittle. I wanted to kill him and regretted I hadn't. I wanted to kill every man who insulted a woman like that . . . there it was again. I hadn't dreamed it. Under the floorboards the tinderbox was rattling.

The town clock had struck three when the man appeared. At first he was nothing more than a vague outline emerging as if from the fabric of the chair opposite my bed, but bit by bit the apparition became solid until, with sinking heart, I recognised the man from the chamber of silver. His white hair, white face glimmered in the candle light. In his hand he held the belt.

'What do you want of me?' I whispered into the inky darkness.

Slowly he rose to his feet.

I pushed myself as far back in the bed as possible. I fair mounted the pillows until there was nowhere else to go. Oh Lord, I thought, he is going to kill me.

He glided across the floor towards me. He was so close that I could have touched him. I could hardly breathe, fear wiped all movement from me and ice-cold sweat ran

down my forehead. He bent and whispered in my ear.

'Master,' he said, 'what is it that you desire?'

I was falling from a great height, and no matter how hard I tried, my eyes refused to open.

I woke to furious banging and for a moment I had no idea where I was or what time it could be.

'Sir, sir,' came the urgent voice of the innkeeper. 'Are you all right?'

'Yes,' I managed, uncertain if that was true or not.

I clambered out of bed and opened the door.

Sir, have you forgotten? The tailor is here with your clothes and the barber is waiting to shave you.'

I tried to clear my head of last night's visitor, to make sense of the group of people standing in the hallway. The innkeeper threw open the curtains and a cold blue light flooded the room.

As if this was the cue they had been waiting for, the tailor's two apprentices entered, one laden with clothes, the other carrying a long, framed mirror over which hung a drape of thick velvet. The tailor followed and immediately went about organising where everything should be placed while I allowed myself to be prodded and pruned back into life by the barber. The tailor went silently to work until at last, with the cloak in position, he was satisfied with my appearance. It was only then, with a flourish worthy of a magician, that he whisked the shroud from the mirror.

I was looking at an awkward young man in a cloak. A

cloak that had so much to it that it could have been easily employed as a sail.

'Perhaps,' I said, holding up each end of the garment, 'it might help if there was a little less of it?'

'Sir,' said the tailor, 'you must wear your cloak with confidence, as becomes a gentleman of your rank. After all, it shows you to be a man of wealth. Let not the cloak wear you.' He demonstrated his meaning. 'It needs to be thrown over the shoulder . . . like so.'

I did as instructed and did not tell him that I felt a fool. He stood back to admire his handiwork, squinting as if I might look better blurred.

'Sir,' said the tailor after a considerable pause. 'Your hat.' I duly put it on and further waited his verdict. 'A cavalier, if ever I saw one,' he said.

The feather in my hat stood upright. It was the only thing I felt I could point out as wrong. With one snip of the tailor's scissors, one stitch of his needle, the feather lay resigned to its flightless fate.

I put on the gloves and stared again into the mirror. I hardly knew who I was. A hollow creature, my self lost in this splendour of finery. It was then that it came to me. I must mimic my captain who tricked people into believing him to be an honourable man and hid well the truth that he was nothing more than a gambler and a drunkard.

I studied the fine young man who looked back at me from the mirror. The clothes, if not he, spoke with confidence. I

stood to attention and again threw my cloak over my shoulder, knocking over a small table in the process.

'There, sir,' said the tailor encouragingly, clapping his hands together. 'You have the gist of it.'

By the time I had practised with the cloak and swaggered up and down the chamber several times to a chorus of flattery, I almost believed I could play the part.

'Your best suit will be here tomorrow,' he assured me. 'And I strongly advise you, sir, that you order another cloak to accompany it.'

I was now fair drunk on my newly acquired wardrobe and, forgetting all about my nightmares, I paid the tailor extra, and thanked him profusely.

After he had left I spied it. I thought that the tailor must have dropped a thimble or such like and was about to pick it up when the town bells rang, not marking the hour but more a warning and there were cries down below. I had gone to look out the window when I was startled by another knock on my bedroom door. There stood the innkeeper. He looked as solemn as a sermon on a Sunday.

'There has been an attack, sir.'

'An attack?' I said. 'By mercenaries?' for I couldn't think what he was talking about.

The innkeeper bent to pick up whatever it was the tailor had dropped.

'Sir,' he said, straightening up, 'the war wouldn't come here, for this dukedom is known to be cursed by werewolves.'

'Have you ever seen them?' I asked.

'No, thank the good Lord,' replied the innkeeper. 'But there are many hereabouts who will swear they have.' He paused. 'Do you mind my asking, sir, how it was you travelled through the forest without being attacked?'

'I don't know,' I said for I had no wish to tell him what had befallen me on the road.

'Did you by chance see anything there?'

'No. Just a lot of trees.'

'Then you are blessed, sir,' said the innkeeper.

His spit-roasted face had a grey quality to it.

'What's happened?'

'It was outside the town, in a farm beyond the river. The farmer and his wife were killed.'

The commotion, the bells, the shouting drew us both to the window. We watched as into the market square came a wagon, its wheels leaving a heavy tread in the snow. On board were two bodies, their wounds clear to see. The town crier was there with the bailiff, who declared that this indeed was a werewolf attack.

Something wasn't right, of that I was certain. I closed the shutters. What trickery was this? Had I not seen what a wolf could do? And all of it more powerful, more terrifying than the marks that lay upon these two dead souls.

'It would be best if you stay here,' said the innkeeper. He went to the door. 'Oh – this must be yours. A strange trophy of war, sir.'

And on the table he put the metal nose. I stared horrified
at it, tried and failed to find my balance, to make some logical
argument as to how the metal nose of the dead soldier should
turn up here in my chamber. Fear like a malignant disease
had slowly crept up on me. I knew the source of my illness yet
knew not how to bring about a cure.

Chapter Nineteen

It was later in the day than I had planned when I took my first step outside The Black Eagle. My new boots being slippery of sole, I fell face over arse in the courtyard, scattering hens and feathers. I felt a fool.

'All the clothes in the world, Otto,' I said to myself, 'will not take away the clod from you.'

Regaining my balance with more caution than I would desire, I finally set off. With each step the actor in me gained confidence. My mind was so filled with my nightmares that in the fading light I found that I had strayed to the top of a hill where the torture wheel stood silhouetted against the oncoming night. The bones of its last victim shone eerily, shreds of clothes blew in the wind. Why was I so plagued by horror?

After much walking and many wrong turns I came to a tavern not far from the castle. I had ordered a beer before I realised my mistake. The tavern was filled with the same motley crew of labourers that I had met the day before. The lavishness of my dress and the folly of my cloak – which I had far from mastered – made me conspicuous. I stood out, a garish bauble in the cruddy filth. Quickly I drank my dark beer and left.

A group of men from the tavern followed. Having no idea which way to go I hastily climbed some stone steps in the hope that the lane might lead me back to the market square. It was a dead end and I could go no farther. At the bottom of the steps were the four men, armed with cudgels, sticks and leather straps. One, the crusty fellow from yesterday, recognised me.

'I told you he was a spy,' he shouted.

These bumpkins had no more idea of battle than a gaggle of geese. In my favour was my position above them on the steps. I took off my cloak and threw it, smothering them with a sail of finest wool. While they tried to untangle themselves I leapt over their backs and ran off the way I had come.

That was when I saw her. The girl in the red cloak. I ran after her, yet for all my speed I couldn't catch up with her and by and by my courage melted. I stopped. So did she. Only then did I realise that the loggerheads were close on my heels. The girl turned towards me but before I could see her face, a door suddenly opened and a lantern shone from one of the houses. A man took my arm and I, half-blinded by the light, fought to free myself. 'Master Hundebiss, we meet again,' said the familiar voice of my saviour of the crossroads. I let myself be pulled inside and quickly the Gentleman of Ragged Order closed the door. My pursuers could be heard shouting as they ran past, then all was silent.

The Gentleman of Ragged Order took me into the kitchen, a room with low, brown-smoked ceilings, wooden beams and the wealth of a well-made fire. It was, so he said, the only chamber that had the hospitality of warmth. From a corner cupboard he brought out a bottle of wine and two glasses.

'I thank you, sir,' I said. 'That's twice you've saved me.'

'Think nothing of it,' he said. 'I'm pleased that this uncomely companion can be of service.' He looked me up and down. 'I see now you are a gentleman, newly minted.'

'More a fool in clothes that I do not think I will ever grow into.'

He chuckled, drank his wine and took tobacco from his pouch. He slowly filled his pipe, studying me all the while.

'You should be careful of this town, for there are people here who are looking for someone to blame for the werewolf attacks. A stranger has a good neck on which to hang the noose of suspicion. I should know, having had the misfortune to be regarded as a stranger for some eleven years. My only regret is that I've never left.'

'What has kept you?' I asked.

'Love,' he said. 'Love is all that keeps anyone anywhere.'

The kitchen door opened and the tallest woman I had ever seen came in, her head near touching the beams.

153

'May I introduce Mistress Dagmar Kurz,' said the Gentleman of Ragged Order, rising to give the giantess a kiss as she put her basket on the table. 'My sun in the eternal winter of my days.'

Mistress Kurz had a strong face and soft eyes, and a warmth in her bearing that drew one close.

'Enough, enough,' said the good mistress. The Gentleman of Ragged Order, taking no heed, threw his arm round her waist. She bent over him and kissed him on the top of his head.

'So this is the infamous Master Hundebiss,' she said.

She turned to put a pot on the stove while my companion related my misadventure. I could see that she was only half-listening and I stood up, thinking that it might be best to take my leave.

She said, 'Sit down, Master Hundebiss. Won't you eat with us?'

Despite all that had happened since I'd left The Black Eagle I had been dreading returning to my chamber. The comfort of the kitchen, the wine, the company and the smell of food did much to make me stay.

'Did you sell anything today?' asked the Gentleman of Ragged Order, bringing more wine to the table.

'No,' said Mistress Kurz. 'Hardly a soul dares venture out. There have been sightings of the werewolves again in a village not far from here – or so I'm told.'

'What do you sell?' I asked, the subject making me uncomfortable.

'Spices, herbal remedies, tokens for lovers, magic charms, stones and jewels to keep evil away. Webs to catch nightmares . . . you must come to my shop, Master Hundebiss.'

'I would very much like to. And please, my name is Otto. Call me Otto.'

She had a wisdom about her and I understood why the Gentleman of Ragged Order had not travelled on. She stooped as she brought the stew to the table, then sat down herself and served the food onto pewter plates.

'You came through the forest,' she said. 'What did you find there?'

'Nothing,' I lied.

The Gentleman of Ragged Order said, 'It matters little if you choose to tell the truth or not. My beloved always knows.'

'All men carry their days upon them,' she said.

We ate in silence until the Gentleman of Ragged Order said, 'Otto, did you see the bodies of the farmer and his wife when they were brought into the market square?'

'Yes, I did. Their injuries looked to be inflicted by a large dog.'

'I thought so too,' said the Gentleman of Ragged Order. 'The town is riddled with fear. Chins wag, loose, lazy tongues spread nothing but hocus pocus. My advice, Otto, is that you leave tomorrow, before the duke is persuaded that the gibbet could use another outing. After all, there is nothing like watching torture to make one appreciate a wedding.'

'A wedding,' I said, feeling coldness sink into my heart.

'The news is everywhere,' said Mistress Kurz. 'Tomorrow Lady Safire is to be betrothed to the prince. The wedding will take place within a matter of days.'

The Gentleman of Ragged Order and Mistress Kurz begged me stay, insisting that it was not safe to be out in the town so late. But the news of Safire's betrothal had wound me up tighter than a Swiss clock, movement being the only remedy for it. They gave me directions to The Black Eagle and I set off, my mind in a whirl. I had no doubt that Safire's wedding gown would be a shroud in which to bury her, that the church bells would mark her final days before the duchess murdered her. I walked through deserted streets, noting that the town had no dogs, for no dog barked. I thought I heard not one sound. Perhaps a latch clicking open somewhere, that was all.

By the time I reached The Black Eagle I had decided what I would spend my cursed gold on. I would buy a carriage and horses and take Safire far, far away from here.

The courtyard was in darkness and to my surprise I found the back door open and cursed the innkeeper for not leaving one lantern for me to see by. Blindly I made my way up the creaking stairs to my chamber. With each tread fear returned to me. I dreaded what I would find when I unlocked my door. Would the dismembered ghost of the Lady of the Nail be hovering, waiting to greet me? As I stood outside my chamber I heard a sound.

When someone spoke in an altogether too human voice I quickly put the key in the lock. There was no need. The door swung open of its own accord. In the moonlight I saw a man, his face masked, my knapsack slung across his back. I rushed at him, my dagger drawn, not realising he had two accomplices waiting in the shadows.

I was punched hard in the ribs and fell to the ground with an almighty thud. A chair came crashing down on me. I thought that the noise would bring the innkeeper running, unless he, his wife and maid had already been slaughtered in their beds. But for all the rumpus, no one came.

I managed to wound one of my assailants, of that much I was sure, for he leapt back clutching his arm and left the fight to his comrades. Now I had two villains to deal with and such was my fury that I lashed out wildly. One had a cudgel and he knocked my knife from me then they both grabbed hold of me and punched me in the stomach so that I bent double. I felt a blow on the side of my head, knew the chamber to be spinning. Consciousness lost its grip.

Chapter Twenty

I was naked, my clothes and boots stolen, my head too painful to lift and my body too bruised to move. The innkeeper was looking down on me as if I were a crocodile washed up in his best chamber.

'Sir, what has happened here?' he asked.

'I've been robbed,' I said, with some difficulty. My tongue felt twice the size it had been.

'Balderdash,' said his wife. 'I told you, husband, he serves the covenant of the werewolf and that is werewolf blood on the stairs.' Her voice was so penetrating that it alone was unbearable to my broken head. 'It was he who bit the butcher.'

Butcher? What was the woman babbling about?

Ignoring what she had to say, I rose slowly to my feet.

'Surely,' I said, 'you heard all the noise. Are you deaf?'

Marie stood at the door, looking at me with interest.

'Have you no work in the kitchen?' said the innkeeper, shooing her out of the chamber.

Embarrassed by my nakedness, he took off his apron and threw it at me.

'What, husband?' said his wife, protesting. 'Do you not think I have seen Adam as he stood before our Lord in all his glory?'

I could not be bothered with any of it. My gold gone, my plan ruined. I looked for my satchel with the dice given to me by the half-beast half-man, only to discover I was the proud owner of nothing, not one gold coin to my name, not one. It all been taken.

The innkeeper was a little shamefaced.

'I heard something, sir,' he said, 'and I thought it was a werewolf.'

I raised my hands to my head.

'Oh Lord, give me strength,' I said.

'Does this mean,' enquired the innkeeper, '. . . does this mean that sir has no money with which to pay for his lodgings?'

Even in my pathetic state I thought I heard a note of glee in his voice.

'Yes, it does,' I said.

'Well then, you will have to piss off.'

'No,' I said. 'I paid to stay in this grand chamber for one week, no less.'

'Ah,' said the innkeeper, 'but that was before we added the clean sheets and meals.'

162

My head hurt so badly that to put together two thoughts that might be related was proving hard to impossible. Then the innkeeper's wife let out a terrible scream. It pierced my head as good as a knife.

'What is it now, wife?' said the innkeeper.

'There – there in the bed!' she shouted. 'The head of a man.'

She pressed herself against the wall, so terrified by things real or imagined that she twisted the corners of her skirt and stuffed the ends into her mouth.

'There's nothing there,' I said firmly, not at all sure that I was right.

'Wife, calm yourself,' said the innkeeper.

'But I saw it, the head of a dead man – wearing a ruff covered in blood. I told you we should never let in strangers. They  bring the devil's work with them.'

'Hold that fat tongue of yours, mistress,' said the innkeeper. 'In these days of war and wolves, we're lucky if we're brought any trade at all.' He went to the bed and pulled back the eiderdown. Unlike his wife, he was not a man cursed with the imagination to see such things. 'Look for yourself. What is wrong with you, woman?'

'I saw it,' repeated his wife. 'I swear on Saint Augustine that I saw the head of a dead man wearing a bloodied ruff, just as I see you standing before me. I swear it on all the saints and my sweet mother's grave.'

I didn't doubt her for a moment.

The innkeeper put his hands on his hips.

'This kind of talk,' he said, 'belongs to tales of witchcraft.'

'It's all your fault, husband – you should never have allowed him to stay here.'

She ran from the room.

I was saved from being thrown out onto the street completely naked by the arrival of the tailor delivering my best suit and cloak. The tailor no doubt had often seen the fortunes of his clients rise and fall within a matter of days. He said he would exchange the suit for something a little more fitting to my position. I demanded that he refund me the difference in cost.

'Sir,' he said, 'this suit was made to fit you and therefore cannot easily be resold.'

I wanted silence and for the innkeeper and the tailor to go away and let me lick my wounds in peace. I was so cold that my teeth had started to chatter. All I could think about was being warm and lying down.

'I want my money returned, tailor, and as for you, innkeeper, what kind of fool leaves his courtyard door open? Did you invite the robbers in? Ah, I will have justice. What are you all? A rabblement of rascals? Is there not an honest man among you?'

The tailor, who prided himself on being an upstanding member of the community, quickly changed his tune. An apprentice was sent to bring me a simple doublet, a shirt, breeches and hose, but alas, no boots. The money I had paid yesterday for the second cloak was also duly returned.

The innkeeper, his spit-roasted face now burned to a crisp, agreed that I was owed at least four more days in the best chamber which translated into two weeks' stay in a freezing cold attic at the very top of the inn.

'Just board, nothing more,' said the innkeeper, 'No meals, one candle.'

As I stood there in my stockinged feet my only consolation was that at least I would be leaving the tinderbox entombed beneath the floorboards of the innkeeper's best chamber.

My new chamber was in the curve of the inn roof, where the tiles were given to rattling in the wind. It possessed one window that looked onto the tops of the houses and beyond the walls of the town to the countryside.

I lay on my straw mattress and felt utterly bereft – all my dreams robbed from me, my hard-won gold stolen before I had a chance to put it to good use. What had I to show? Nothing but a humble suit of clothes and this hovel of a room. Who was responsible for my downfall? I went through the list of

suspects: Krempel the gold merchant, the innkeeper, his wife, Marie . . . ? I laughed. I had only myself to blame.

'What a hero you are, Otto,' I said. 'What a dunce. You should have taken better care of your wealth.'

It was later that day when the town bailiff puffed and wheezed his way up the spindly stairs. The innkeeper trailed behind him. The bailiff pushed open the door and his shape took up most of the space. He studied me carefully and prodded me with his staff.

'You claim you have been robbed,' he said.

'Yes,' I replied. 'And assaulted.'

He moved back the moth-eaten eiderdown with the tip of his staff to have a better look at me.

'Hmm,' he said. 'When did this happen?'

'Last night,' said the innkeeper.

'Last night. You had just returned to the inn?'

'Yes. I had been . . . '

Then I thought better of saying where I had been, knowing it to be pointless and more likely than not to bring trouble upon the Gentleman of Ragged Order and his mistress. I put my arm over my eyes. This would be a long-winded farce.

'Last night, Master Hundebiss,' said the bailiff, 'there was a werewolf attack. The butcher's boy was near mauled to death.'

'I'm sorry to hear it,' I said.

'Hmm. Since you arrived there have been three attacks by werewolves. People are beginning to talk and wag their fingers in your direction.'

I removed my arm to look at him and with difficulty sat up.

'Are you suggesting that I had something to do with the attacks?'

The bailiff had an itchy look about him.

'I tell you this, sir. If anything else suspicious happens in these parts then you will be thrown into the keep and brought to trial.'

'Me? I'm the one who has been robbed. You, sir, should be out looking for the villains instead of standing here questioning a wounded man.'

The bailiff rubbed his nose, a large bulbous thing, and said in the same measured tone as before, 'The innkeeper's wife tells me you have a mark on your shoulder in the shape of a wolf.'

'What?'

'Such markings belong to sorcery.'

'Leave me alone,' I shouted. 'Just leave me alone, both of you. If you can't find the villains who did this then don't bother me. Out! Get out!'

I lay down and closed my eyes, half-expecting to be dragged off to prison. Instead both men, knowing they stood on shaky ground, retreated.

If it had not been for Marie I might well have frozen to death up there. She brought me soup and bread, and smuggled in an extra quilt for warmth. By the second day I felt less given to stiffness and soreness of head.

She appeared late that morning full of gossip from the castle. Her best friend worked as a serving maid for the duke. The night before, the duke had held a banquet to celebrate his daughter's betrothal to the prince.

My heart sank.

'How was the Lady Safire?' I asked.

The how of Lady Safire lay in what she wore, according to Marie's friend. It was the latest fashion from the Netherlands. A full slashed sleeve finished just above the elbow, the bodice high on the waist, low at the shoulders, edged with lace and tied round the middle with ribbon. The skirt, not wide, was pulled back so that her gold petticoat could be seen. As for the fabric of the cloth, Marie's friend thought it was watered silk, the colour of ochre.

'Marie, enough. I want to know how she looked.'

'And I have told you. Pale skin, hair styled in soft curls.'

'No, no – did she look happy or sad?'

'Why, she looked the same as many a maiden when betrothed.'

'And what is that?'

'Sad, sir. My friend thought she had sad eyes. Nevertheless it was quite an occasion. It must have been a bit of a shock, when you think of all those years she has been locked away, to come out to such grandeur. My friend said the duchess was green with jealousy.'

I could see that it was hopeless to ask anything more but

once started on a subject Marie was loath to finish.

'The wedding is to take place in four days' time. So my friend says.'

'Four days!' I said, sitting bolt upright. 'Why so soon?'

'I don't know everything,' said Marie, 'do I?'

I reached for breeches. Somehow I had to stop the wedding.

'Sir,' said Marie, alarmed. 'What are you doing?'

'I am going out,' I said and stood up so suddenly that I remember nothing else.

Chapter Twenty-One

I am with my sister. It is summer and we are walking together, singing, accompanied by the buzz of bees. In a basket she is carrying are the strawberries we have collected. The meadow grass is tall and the wind blows through it. In the distance is a church steeple. We run, laughing, to a wooden gate nestled in a copse of trees. Suddenly I know that we must turn back and I pull at her. 'There is nothing to be afraid of,' she says. The wicker gate closes behind us.

It is then that we see them lying there,
the hens pluck-pluck-plucking at their limbs,
their clothes, their eyes. All the people from our
village, dead. My sister puts down the basket of
strawberries and carefully starts removing their
shoes. I watch as she collects them.
Finally, my sister sits on the ground and takes
off her own shoes. I am screaming, 'Don't do
that, please don't.'
She takes no notice. She picks up an armful
of her strange fruit and walks away from me
and I know who she is walking towards.
I know and I cannot look, for if I do I will
see the half-beast half-man and I won't give
him my soul. I won't.

I lay miserable in the dark while images of my dead sister danced before me. I longed for a spark of fire, a match, a light to ease my grief. Night is an unforgiving time; it makes the horror of dreams last longer until you can't tell where dreaming ends or waking begins, and both seem as unreal as the other.

The town hall clock rang midnight and on the last chime I heard a distant scouring sound. Just the wind, tumbling through the timbers. But by degrees it came closer. Whatever it was sounded as if it was climbing the stairs towards me.

Was I awake? Was I asleep? I sat up and stared desperately into that darkness, trying not to make monsters of the shapes I saw, telling myself they were only old boxes and rubbish that the innkeeper stored there. I heard a mouse skittling between some sacks.

'There's nothing here,' I said. The moon languidly appeared from behind a cloud and shone in at my window, throwing a patch of light on the dusty floor beside me.

'See, Otto,' I said. 'The room is empty. It's the tail end of nightmares, nothing more.'

I lay back down, determined to sleep, but the moon was rudely snuffed out by a passing cloud and all was pitch black. There it was again, that noise. Louder it grew, until my door was blown open by its breath.

'Who's there?' I called. 'Who are you?'

Not a sound.

Yet someone had entered the room. I could feel their presence, smell dog-wet fur.

I dared not move. A scream, jagged as a knife, pinned me to the bed.

'What do you want?' I hissed into the abyss.

Not a word.

'Speak!' I shouted. 'I know you are there.'

I heard the gravel growl of a great beast.

173

I do not know how long I lay there, the scream finally tearing its way into my throat, my eiderdown stuffed into my mouth. Terrified, wide-eyed, I watched the shadows. Out of the darkness they came and stood at the end of my bed: the first soldier I had ever killed, a gaping hole where once his face had been. He was followed by the ghosts of all those I had slain, each holding a candle to wounds still freshly bleeding, each whispering his name before his candle went out.

Cold with loathing, I recalled my life, my loss, and hoped no more apparitions would come to torment me. It was quiet except for the wheezing of my unwanted companion.

'Let me have a light,' I begged. 'Let me see who you are.'

For a moment I thought my wish had been heard for a lantern globe came towards me, bobbing up and down. Who held it, I could not see and suddenly I knew I did not want to see. She was here too, the Lady of the Nail, her face masked, her neck bloody, teeth marks still upon it. She glided towards me. In her other hand she carried a white velvet cushion on which her thumbnail rested, curled in upon itself. She bent down and I could smell her corpse-like breath.

'Now the eye of me sees all too well,' she whispered. 'Know you not your power?'

Then the hag from hell was gone. The scream in me remained, my mind losing its anchor on reason. The clock on the town hall sounded the passing hours, time wearily dragging its iron feet across the night. On the last stroke of five

I breathed again for whoever my companion had been, he left
that hour. If he was man or beast I could not tell.

I watched the reluctant day dawn and persuaded
myself that it had been a nightmare, no worse than many
a nightmare I had had before.

I propped myself up and looked round the
attic room.
All was as it should be.

Except nothing was as it should
be. I knew in that second that the
tinderbox would never leave me.
It lay on top of my clothes as
if it had always been there.
I wrapped the eiderdown
round me and put my
bare feet on the
frozen, frosted
floor.

Cautiously, I picked it up. Was I never to be free of this cursed thing? For a reason I did not understand it was by some supernatural power contracted to me, for neither had fire destroyed it, nor had burial prevented it finding its way back.

I had often seen my captain wake with a sore head and swear he would never drink again, only to be tempted back to the bottle as soon as his head would allow.

'It owns me, does that bloody bottle,' he once said. 'I'm its tragic servant, not its master.'

I held the tinderbox and thought his words well described how I felt. My mouth was dry as I lifted the lid. What did I expect to find inside? The devil's heart? It was in truth no different from any other tinderbox. Here was the steel, here the flint, here the tinder.

Slowly, very slowly, I reached for the candle by my bed. I took a deep breath, held the steel in my hand and with its sharp edge I struck a spark of fire from the flint.

Before me was the man with the dog-black hair and in his gloved hand he held his belt.

'Master,' he said. 'What is it that you desire?'

I looked down at the tinderbox and then up at the man from the chamber of bronze. It took me a while to trust what I was seeing. Then by degrees the scream in me found voice.

'Is it you? Are you the reason the tinderbox haunts me? For the Lord's sake, tell me why.'

'My brothers and I are free until the tinderbox finds a master. You struck the flint.'

'So that is why the Lady of the Nail wanted it.'

'You struck the flint once and I came. If you strike it twice my brother from the chamber of silver will appear.'

I hardly dared speak. 'Three times?'

'My brother from the chamber of gold.'

He stood there still, his dead eyes upon me.

'Master, what is it that you desire?' he repeated.

I had nothing to lose.

'I desire to have my gold returned to me, to be warm, and to eat.'

In a glimmer, he was gone and I wondered then if my mind might not be slipping into madness.

Chapter Twenty-Two

Later that morning the innkeeper came rushing up the stairs calling, 'Sir, sir!'

He pushed open the attic door. 'Sir, come quickly: it is nothing short of a miracle. Your possessions have all been returned.'

In my stockinged feet I followed him down to the parlour, to find Marie and the innkeeper's wife staring at my knapsack.

'There's blood on it,' said Marie, a look of awe on her face.

Blood or no blood, I picked it up. It was pleasingly heavy. Inside was all my gold, even the purse with the money in it, not a coin spent.

Beside it was a basket with my clothes and boots. On top was my satchel and inside were my dice. In fact everything that had been taken from me the night of the robbery.

'How did this arrive here?' I asked.

'I don't know, sir,' said the innkeeper. 'I thought there was a fox in the yard, for the din that the hens were making. When I opened the door I found this sitting there.'

Relief washed over me.

'Witchcraft,' muttered his wife. 'That is what it is.'

'I doubt that,' I said, louder than I had intended. 'More likely someone had a bad conscience.'

The innkeeper hastened to assure me he had nothing to do with the matter.

'Witchcraft,' repeated his wife. 'And sorcery. I can see the devil's hand upon it.'

The innkeeper turned on her.

'You can see this and you can see that, and all of it gibberish, woman. Sir, forgive me,' he babbled, and for a moment I thought he was about to confess to the robbery. 'I acted in a state of shock when I thought you had no money, so to speak, and I was this very morning going to say you must have your room back. Wasn't I, wife?'

'Ye-es,' she said, unsure if that was the right or the wrong of it.

'Plus the adjoining room, a well-trimmed chamber.'

I was so tired, cold and hungry that I said, 'But first I want breakfast. And coffee, yes, hot coffee.'

'Coffee,' said the innkeeper's wife. 'A sorcerer's brew if ever there was.'

'Wife – hold that fat tongue of yours. Marie – coffee.'

Never had I seen the three of them move faster. By midday I had been installed in my two chambers with a roaring fire and had dined like a king. The tailor had all too willingly returned my best suit and cloak.

For the first time in days I was warm, could think clearly, and only then did the magnitude of my discovery dawn on me. I was master of the tinderbox, and if that was so, what more could I wish for but to free Safire and take her away from here?

I needed air, to walk, to think. But where to hide the knapsack and the tinderbox? Quietly, I mounted the stairs to the attic and pushed open the door. Under the boxes and sacks I hid my treasure.

Sallow of face, nose aglow, the bailiff appeared as I was on the verge of leaving the inn.

'Master Hundebiss.'

'Yes?' I said. 'I am going out.'

He was a large man and the bulk of him made leaving impossible, for he blocked the door completely.

'Where were you last night?'

'Up there in that miserable attic.'

'And did you ever leave the attic?'

'No. How could I? I had no boots. Do you think I grew wings?'

It struck me then that some sudden mischief had occurred and whatever it was had so shocked the bailiff that he was on the verge of fainting.

I grabbed hold of his arm to steady him, took him to a chair and pushed his head between his legs, a trick that had always worked well with my captain. I called to the innkeeper for cognac and glancing up saw that the courtyard was full of people.

'What has happened?' I asked, almost certain that I did not want to know.

'There has been a . . . a . . . werewolf attack,' said the bailiff, raising his head. 'But this is unlike any there have been before.'

'Who was attacked?'

'Master Krempel and his two clerks.' He paused. 'Hardly anything is left of them . . . just . . . bits.'

And with that he ran to the door and vomited.

In the crowded courtyard a woman shouted, 'When will the curse be lifted?'

'They are bringing them into the market square,' called another, and the crowd moved in a wave from the courtyard.

All the relief of having my gold back, of finding myself master of the tinderbox faded. This was the price: the murder of its thieves, and I wished it was not so.

Chapter Twenty-Three

The crowd that had gathered outside the inn was a hostile bunch and whether innocent or guilty I was seen as the main cause of their unrest. At dusk the duke's guards marched into the market square and reluctantly the good citizens of the town dispersed.

I had spent the day in my chamber by the blazing fire. With the tinderbox had come might undreamed of, that made my wealth but a garish trinket. What was it that I desired? One thing only. Safire.

It was midnight when I took the lantern and went silently to the attic, listening for any movement, for I did not want my hiding place to be discovered. At the top of the house where the shadows lived and shapes took on the appearance of monsters my nerve almost failed me, but desire for the tinderbox had taken hold and at that moment I would have

fought any man for it. Such was its
power.

Once back safe in my
chambers I placed the tinderbox
on the table. It was as inevitable as
night follows day.

Two strikes of the steel and
there he was, the man from the
chamber of silver. Taller than his
brother, leaner, his hair white, his
blue eyes frosted. He shimmered
like a reflection caught in a
mirrored glass. In his hand he held
his belt.

'Master,' he said. 'What is it
that you desire?'

His eyes never left mine.
And as with the half-beast half-
man I felt as if he already knew
my thoughts and saw the darkest
corner of me, yet judged me not.

'For the Lady Safire to be
brought to me,' I said.

No sooner had the words left
my mouth than all the candles blew
out.

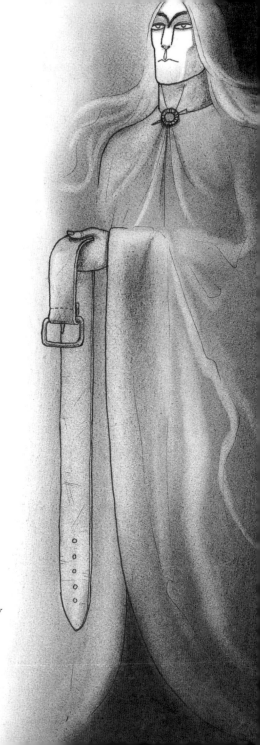

'I will kill you,' I hear a voice
say into the darkness. 'So help me,
I will kill you.'

The candles rekindle and there
she is in a muslin gown, her hair all
fiery red, her eyes aflame. I am struck
stupid by the sight of her for she is
perfect in every way, her face more
lovely than I remember.

She comes towards me, a dagger
pointed at my heart. Should I be afraid?
I know I am not. What afears me most
is the thought that she might vanish just
as suddenly as she appeared.

I try to grab hold of her hand
in the hope that she will drop the
knife. Her hand pulls free from
mine. I feel a burning pain
on my cheek and blood
trickles into my mouth.

'I am Otto,' I say. 'Remember? Otto?'

She is not listening. I try to push her away and still she comes at me like a wild cat.

'You tell the prince . . .' she says.

The knife cuts my hand. The sight of the blood makes her recoil and the knife clatters to the floor. Quickly I put my foot over it.

'Tell the prince,' she says, backing away from me, 'that I would rather murder him than marry him. He might as well make my wedding gown into a hangman's rope.'

'I am Otto,' I say again. 'We met in a tree.'

'Otto?' she says looking up at me, her breath coming fast. Her gown has fallen from her shoulder.

'Otto,' she says, as if seeing me for the first time.

'Yes.'

'You had a hen.'

'I did indeed.'

'What are you doing here?' she says. 'Are you one of the prince's spies?'

'No, no!'

'Tell me I am dreaming, for there is blood on your hand and your cheek. I fear I have wounded you. But a moment ago, or so it seemed, the prince was in my chamber.'

'Perhaps we are both asleep,' I say, 'and have met by chance in our dreams.'

'I think you may well be right,' she says, touching my cheek and the warmth of her hand makes us both jump. 'Did I do this?'

The chamber has undergone a transformation. The drapes that were once of dusty, mouse-bitten brocades are now the finest tapestries. As for my humble bed, it is a throne of a four-poster. The adjoining chamber is no less ornate. It is wood-panelled and in the centre a huge chandelier hangs over a round table bathed in candlelight, laid with flowers, fruits and wine. Music fills the air.

'My lord,' says Safire and curtseys. 'Is this your castle?'

I cannot think what to say.

'Why, you must be wealthier than the prince.' Her face lights up with laughter. 'Otto, you are a magician.'

I suppose I am. I have the power of the tinderbox at my command. We drink the wine and eat the fruit and she speaks

190

of the mother she never knew.

'Castle walls broke her spirit . . .

' . . . the court weakened her mind.

'She died the night I was born.

'My brothers counted me as one of them . . .

' . . . I climbed trees and garden walls.

'I had no fear of heights.

'When they left the whole world floated into the sea to drown.

'They are alive.

'I cannot leave here until they return.'

I put my hand out to touch hers.

'You too are cast in sadness thicker than stone, heavier than water,' she says. 'It ties you, like me, to this leaden earth.'

I lean forward and kiss her.

'Only in dreams,' she says, 'can we be ourselves, uncaged, wild of spirit. Here I am free to climb a tree and find a boy with eyes as sad as mine.'

There is so much I want to tell her but my words all tangle in on themselves. Instead I watch her as she dances slowly round the chamber.

She asks me, 'Is it possible to fall in love with someone in your dreams?'

'Yes,' I say, 'Oh, yes.'

Chapter Twenty-Four

At five in the morning the market clock chimed and I was alone, all the trappings of grandeur vanished. Was it a dream? How could a dream feel so real, have a scent to it, carry weight?

The tinderbox was there, on the table. I laughed out loud.

Tonight I would have her brought to me again. I am a prince. No, a king. Never had the world looked as good or the day as giddy-bright as it did that morning. Of all the many extraordinary things that had happened to me, Safire was the most extraordinary. I had no need to worry about her wedding or my safety, for I could at any moment summon the werewolves to spirit us away. But a thought struck me. She would not leave the town until her brothers were home.

I had the answer. I would strike the tinderbox and, if they were still alive, have them brought back.

I had become king of the dim-witted for I believed that life was simple.

I heard the innkeeper moving about and, closing my eyes, fell fast asleep.

Later that morning, after I'd dressed, I rolled the dice, expecting to throw four Jacks and a ten that would tell me to stay. To my surprise I rolled four Jacks and a nine, meaning I should travel west.

I would not listen to their wisdom, not today. I put them away in my satchel and, with a heart full of love for mankind, went in search of Mistress Kurz's shop. I had an idea to give Safire a token of some sort so that when she woke she would know that what had passed was not a dream.

The shop was tucked away off the market square. The goods in the window drew my attention. Puppets dangled below a multitude of curiosities, lit by candles so they twinkled as a magic cave might. I pushed the door, a bell rang and from the back came Mistress Kurz.

'Otto,' she said. 'I have been expecting you.'

I looked around, wondering at the jars on the cabinets and the bunches of herbs hanging from the ceiling.

'I suspect you are not here for medicine,' she said, 'but for a love token.'

I studied a tray of trinkets she showed me. It glowed with all things red: a bird feather, pebbles, shells from distant shores, dried roses, a blown egg, a phial of sand, an unpolished stone.

As I wondered which to buy, Mistress Kurz took from a drawer a gold ring made for the most delicate of fingers and set with a ruby as fiery as Safire's spirit.

'This stone could tell you many a tale,' she said. 'It is the colour of passion, the colour of fire, the colour of blood.'

I held it up to the light. I knew it was made for my Safire.

'I will take it,' I said. 'How much?'

She charged me a price well within my means.

She wrapped it in silk and handing it to me, said that the Gentleman of Ragged Order wanted to speak to me urgently.

She closed the shop, and together we walked towards the river. The Gentleman of Ragged Order came towards us, his arm raised in greeting.

'There you are. Good, very good. Let us walk,' he said and steered us in the direction of the ramparts.

Down by the river, where the fishing boats were frozen in the water and a bitter wind moaned from the forest, stood a lopsided tavern. The tavern keeper seemed well-acquainted with the Gentleman of Ragged Order and his mistress and showed us to a room at the back where the fire splattered against the cold. He brought us a jug of beer, sausage and a loaf of bread.

'I told you,' said the Gentleman of

Ragged Order as soon as the tavern keeper had left, 'that this town does not like strangers.'

'I can look after myself.'

'You are in great danger,' said Mistress Kurz. 'Tell him, my love.'

'This town,' said the Gentleman of Ragged Order, 'is suspicious of its own shadow, worried by the sounds of neighbours' footsteps, scared lest the walls have witches' ears. Do you not understand? Even Mistress Kurz – who was born here – is looked upon as a sorceress. Her height alone singles her out. Now, since the werewolf attacks began in the town, people are frightened senseless. The burgher master's finger is itching to point at someone who is not from this place. A stranger has the right shoes, a foreign sort of shoes that fit such a problem as this. The bailiff will not hesitate to arrest you and drag you to the hangman; the hangman will not hesitate to torture you and drag you to the gallows.'

Mistress Kurz said very quietly, 'The Gentleman of Ragged Order will take you away from here tonight.'

'I can't leave,' I said. 'Not yet.'

I thanked them for their concern, but I could only think that the night was drawing in and soon Safire would be brought to me. The rest could wait.

I stood up to say goodbye and assured them I would leave the town soon.

'Soon,' said Mistress Kurz, 'will be too late.'

Chapter Twenty-Five

As I made my way back to The Black Eagle I became
conscious of being followed. He walked not far behind me, his
sword clinking by his side. Every way I turned, there he was.
He clung tight to my shadow and I hoped that was all
he would ever have of me.

   There is a relief in crowds – misguided, I know, for I
have seen whole villages massacred, cut down no less than
corn is in a field and left to rot. I was sure that my shadow-
catcher had no need to mind if a few market stall-holders
saw him make stubble of me. My gamble was on a group of
children playing with a makeshift sledge. I walked purposely
towards them as one of their party broke away and, having
given himself a mighty push, now came hurtling down the
icy cobbles. I moved quickly out of the way and my shadow-
catcher, being slower, took the full force of the collision. In the
confusion of who did what to whom I made my escape.

Inside the inn Marie was clattering on the stone floor with pail and brush while in the main room sat four merchants, slightly the worse for wine.

'I hope the bailiff keeps his word,' said one, 'and arrests the beast before the wedding takes place, and hangs him good and proper.'

'But who is he?' asked his ginger-bearded drinking companion.

'The town council has concluded that he must be a stranger. And the only stranger in this town is . . . Marie!' he called. 'What is the name of your guest?'

I did not stay to hear more but made my way unseen to my chamber and locked my door. I peeped out of the window. The sun had begun to set, defeated in a weeping sky, and my shadow-catcher now stood in the doorway opposite, looking up. I shut the shutters and lay down on the bed. Time was not on my side, and if it was not for the tinderbox I would have thought more on how to escape this cursed place. Instead, I told myself, let them whisper and gossip as much as they like. I had the wealth of Midas, and the power of three mighty wolves at the flick of a flint. There was nothing that was so important that it could not wait until tomorrow.

I took the ring from my pocket and by the firelight examined it. Why should a free spirit such as Safire be tied to the prince who did not love her, who would snuff out the brightness of her flame? It did not strike me then as impossible that we could be together for ever. I closed my eyes.

The sky is so vast above me and I insignificant
beneath it. My sister is standing on the blood-red
waters, calling to me. The noise of musket fire
overwhelms her words. This, then, is goodbye.
I will never reach her.
The puny smallness of me is terrifying.
In the distance two figures emerge from the smoke
of battle. One is hooded. The other, a child in
a red cloak, walks with him. They move with
unnatural speed over the river, past my sister,
and come to a stop beside me.
The child pulls at my doublet and says
in the voice of a grown woman,
'That is my ring you have in your pocket.'
Weeping, I take it out and give it to her.
'My sister,' I say, for all I can hear are the
cries of a drowning woman.
The girl throws the ring into the air.
I want to say, don't, I will lose it. But from her
hands comes a red-breasted bird. It spreads its
wings and flies away until sky and bird are one.
The hooded man turns slowly towards me.
I see his teeth, his eyes. I am looking into
the face of a wolf.

I woke not knowing where I was or who I was and, in that moment, I felt more lost than I had when I knew my family was dead, more tangled than in the forest, more wounded than on the battlefield. Only the weight of the ring in my hand brought me back into myself. Perhaps this stolen love makes nightmares worse.

Safire, Safire, I need to know. I need to hear you say you love me.

If she were to tell me that daylight humiliated all night-time passion, that she could never love one such as I, then I would pack up, take my tinderbox and be gone.

The town hall clock chimed midnight. Fumbling, I struck steel against flint thrice. I knew he was there even before I looked up. The man from the chamber of gold. He shone with the light of a golden autumn.

'Master,' he said. 'What is it that you desire?'

'To have Lady Safire brought to me.'

But he did not move.

I said again, 'Bring Lady Safire to me.'

Still he did not move.

'You had a sister?' he asked me at last.

I was taken aback by his question.

'Yes, I did.'

'You loved her dearly?'

'Yes, I did.'

'Then you know well what a treasured gift a sister is to a brother?'

'I do indeed.'

By degrees he moved closer to me, his eyes seas of golden water.

'Bring to me Safire,' I demanded. 'That is my desire.'

He vanished.

Once again my chamber is changed into sumptuous rooms, filled with rich light that burnishes everything all about, belonging to neither night nor day.

I feel her behind me. She puts her hands over my eyes.

'Who do you think it is?' she whispers. I take her in my arms and kiss her. The nobleman's daughter and the soldier boy, lost in that embrace.

I pull away from her.

'If you were to see me in the light of day,' I ask her, 'would you still want me?'

'I am condemned to a life I do not want with a man I hate,' she says, her face so serious, her eyes so sad. 'Whether this is a dream or not, you are the husband of my soul and for all time will be. Only you can calm the flame of me.'

I take her hand and lead her to the other room. Everything is perfect, or so I think until she sees the three portraits. In their shadow her face falls.

'But these are my three brothers,' she says.

Each painting is of a fine young man. One is dressed in bronze, the second in silver, the third in gold. Behind each is the same background: the forest, dark and brooding.

'Do you know them?' she asks. Her eyes search mine.

'Alas, I don't,' I say, though I am in terror that I might.

She turns back to look at them and all three brothers have vanished from their frames, leaving only the dark forest behind.

'I am dreaming, for I saw them and now they are gone.' As if storm clouds were passing over the face of the sun, she says, 'Do you have the power to bring them home?'

'Hush,' I say. 'Hush. There is more betwixt the day and the night than we can ever know.'

I make her close her eyes. Her eyelashes are so thick and long they flutter as if they might take flight. I take her finger and gently place the ring on it. I feel that my heart has stopped beating.

She opens her eyes.

'I long for you,' she says, and kisses me.

I untie her gown, she unbuttons my doublet, takes off my shirt; her finger traces the wound on my shoulder.

Laughing now we pull off the remains of our clothes before we tumble onto the softness of the bed, our bodies on fire. In that golden light we make love. This night is ours.

I am no longer lost.

No longer old.

The nightmares are gone.

The road curls home.

Chapter Twenty-Six

Long before the cock crowed, Safire vanished as swiftly as
she had arrived and my surroundings once more took on the
humbler appearance of the innkeeper's chambers. I lay in that
happy state between dreams and waking where but a moment
ago Safire had lain beside me.

The early morning light made everything different, as if I
could see where before I had merely looked. I felt drunk on the
wonder of love.

The tinderbox, now my most valuable possession, was by
my side and I was glad of it. It was more precious than all my
gold for it had the power to bring Safire to me.

I sighed into the dew of the new day. My life, so long
void of meaning, had at last found purpose. I determined that
on our wedding day my gift to her would be to set her brothers
free, for I believed with all the beats left in my heart that I

owned fortune enough to put a wrong right. Oh, such are the plans of fools. A wise man knows better than to call fortune his friend.

I struck the flint once. At first I didn't see him hidden in the folds of shadows but heard him say, 'Master, what is it that you desire?'

The man from the chamber of bronze was before me.

'To find out what happened to . . . Safire's brothers. To know how I might set them free.'

My breath was knotted tight within me, and in that moment I knew I didn't want to know the answer.

I waited. Nothing happened and I thanked the gods for it and sure that he had left, I lay on the bed, images of Safire dancing before me. Oh, what joy that name brought me. How long is a day and why is it full of so many useless hours that do naught but worry at a man's soul? Bring on the night and bring Safire back to me.

I am in the forest. Rays of shot silk sun fall between the branches of the trees. Jewelled dragonflies dance over the tall bracken that cloaks the ground. In the heat haze I see three horsemen ride towards me. It is summer and I have forgotten what a multitude of leaves this season holds.

The riders come to a halt under an ancient oak tree. Spangled sunlight catches young, earnest faces. All three swear allegiance to one another, to protect their sister, Safire, to free the dukedom from tyranny. The man from the chamber of bronze is standing by my side. He is my guide to all that I witness.

'The past can only be seen in the shimmer of a dying flame,' he says. 'Here it burns golden, fanned by the winds of regret. That is me.' He points to one of the riders. 'My name is Gerhard. I am eighteen years old. Those are my brothers. They are twins, two years older than I. Gerfried is he with white hair and Gotfrid's hair is golden. We meet here in the forest because we have been banished from the dukedom and forbidden to see our sister again.'

'What is your crime?' I ask.

'We are thorns in the side of our father's new wife, who you, master, call Mistress Jabber. She is a witch by birth though her gifts are but a sneeze compared with those of her sister. The duchess has beauty and has spellbound our father the duke so that he is but a tatterman, a puppet in her hands. She is not content with that. She wants more: to rid the land for ever of my father and his heirs so she and the prince can rule together. With the help of her sister she has conceived a plan.'

The heat wobbles the edges of my vision and it seems all might be consumed by flames.

206

*Soldiers assemble under the trees and from their ranks a
horseman rides towards the brothers. His face is tight as if it
cost too much to give definition to his features. A mean line of a
mouth, a cruelty to him that I am told women call handsome.
I saw this face in the maze.*

*'This,' says my narrator, 'is the prince who swore to help us rid
the land of the duchess and her soldiers. This is the army he raised
with our gold to fight our cause. Here then, we think, is our
salvation.'*

*The three brothers gallop off, the prince leading the way, the
soldiers in their wake. Already they are ghosts in the glimmer of
the heat haze.*

*I follow, not knowing how it is that I am so fast upon their heels.
I overtake them and with such speed that forest, trees and wind
become one.*

*Once more I am standing in the great chamber with its dome of
ice. In this strange summer frost lies upon the stone floor. There
she sits, the Lady of the Nail. Back and forth walks Mistress
Jabber.*

*'My dear sister, it is but a piddling favour, nothing more, that
I request of you. After all, such wealth as you possess needs its
guardians.'*

'Do you think I cannot see through your devious ways?' says the Lady of the Nail. 'Your crooked heart beats a warning as might a drum. Have I not given you a dukedom with lands so vast that the mere walking on them will warm the soles of your feet? Have you not the marriage you set your deep, red heart on?'

'That was before I met the prince.'

'Will you never be satisfied, sister? You have the beauty and charm which was denied me by the wishes of our mother. And yet I am always called upon to do your bidding.'

'Do this for me,' says Mistress Jabber, 'and I will never ask another thing of you, ever. That I promise.'

At those words a lick of flame flicks across the frosted floor.

'Liar,' says the Lady of the Nail. She rises and moves towards her sister, her long thumbnail uncurling. She jabs it into her sister's arm. 'A curse be on you and your prince.'

'Sister! You do not mean that.'

'Oh, but I do,' says the Lady of the Nail. 'A curse be on you both if your stepdaughter does not marry the prince by the time she is seventeen.'

'Why is that so important to you?' asks Mistress Jabber.

The Lady of the Nail laughs. 'Because jealousy will eat away your immortality.'

'What have I done to make you hate me so?'

'Do you not know? Then you are a thick-witted boggle-headed woman. Grimly greedy with no more foresight than the end of your stubbed nose. I tell you this, and evermore it shall be so: you and the prince will both die if she marries anyone else.'

I look up and see that the ice dome is clouded black. It moves as a mass before spiralling downwards. Thousands and thousands of bluebottles reach the ground and break away in swarms that form servants clad in iridescent armour standing guard around the Lady of the Nail.

With a look of disgust on her face Mistress Jabber says, 'So be it.'

The prince enters the chamber followed by soldiers dragging with them the three brothers. They are gagged and their hands bound. A smile curls the prince's thin lips, such is his pride in his captives.

Three belts lie on a cushion. From the ranks of servants the wizened man steps forward. He is holding the tinderbox.

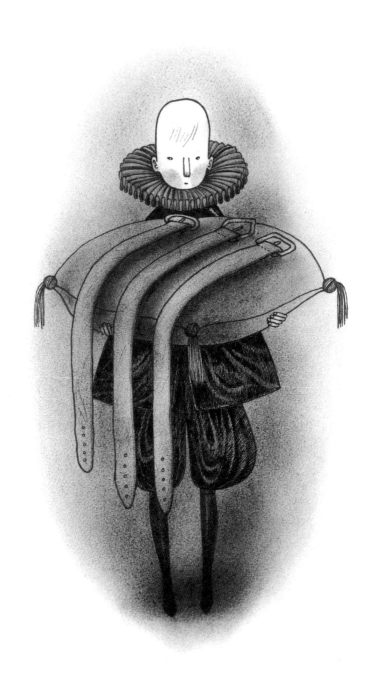

Slowly the Lady of the Nail puts the first belt round Gerhard. All colour drains from his face and his body begins to twist and shudder as if he may well fall asunder. He starts to grow in size; his head and face rapidly lose the look of a man and change by degrees into that of a wolf, his eyes yellow, bright as moonshine. The fabric of his clothes gives way to thick fur, his cloak dissolves into a tail. He snarls, showing teeth as sharp as steel blades his arms and muscles extend, his hands turn into mighty paws. His two brothers watch, horror-struck, as Gerhard disappears and in his place towers a monstrous wolf. The wizened servant gives the tinderbox to the Lady of the Nail. She removes the lid and strikes the flint. As she does so Gerhard disappears. It is Gerfried's turn. The belt causes the same transformation but more slowly this time, drawn out, or so it seems. I see every hair appear from his skin, each one silvery white. His blue eyes shine too brightly and the look of them sends ice into my heart. Taller still is he. Only when full grown does he lunge at the prince with a liquid movement, luscious as velvet. Mistress Jabber screams. Before he can do any harm the Lady of the Nail again strikes the flint, enslaving Gerfried to the tinderbox.

When the last belt is placed round Gotfrid, he lets out a howl of pain. He grows in size until he fills the room, shattering the ice dome. All light is blocked by his bulk and in the darkness I hear a long low sigh, a hiss of air from a corpse. The breath is close to my ear.

Chapter Twenty-Seven

'We desire to have no master, only to protect our father's land and our sister. We would kill rather than give up the belts that were forced upon us. As werewolves our spirits are free of conscience, of morals, of religion; our feeble bodies are replenished. We are cursed with the thirst for blood that no human banquet can ever satisfy.'

The voice of Gerhard, the man from the chamber of bronze, followed me into sudden waking.

I am told that sleep is a rehearsal for death. It is waking that kills us. I made it back to the watery isle of day but carried with me a secret that no sleep could rob me of.

I woke with blood in my mouth, my nose streaming red. I lay back and kept my eyes wide open, not sure that I ever wanted to close them again. Turning my head only slightly to my left I saw that the tinderbox was still there and the dice sat upon the table. I hoped that the sight of them might calm my muddled mind, though I could feel in every bone of me the weight, coffin-heavy, of this unwanted secret. All of me tumbled into the thunder of troubled thought.

I longed to reclaim the simplicity of the night when the world in its magnitude lay at my feet and Safire lay in my arms, when I had in my heart but an innocent wish to free her brothers. Now I knew they were to stay for ever bound to the tinderbox, for the belts were no different from the bottle that my captain couldn't leave alone. If Safire was to be mine I must never tell her what had befallen her brothers.

I waited for the bleeding to stop, then holding a cloth to my nose, I stood up and at that very moment Marie entered the room with a tray, my breakfast upon it. Tray, beer, pewter plates, mug, went flying and landed louder than a drum roll.

'Oh sir!' she screeched. 'You too have been murdered!'

'It's a nose-bleed,' I said. 'Nothing more.' And was about to add, 'What is wrong with you?' when I caught sight of myself in the mirror.

My face was indeed a gory mess, covered in patches of dried blood.

'And your hands, sir,' said Marie. 'Look at your hands.'

It was hopeless. I could hardly convince her that I was alive. Defeated, I slumped in a chair.

'Shall I call for the doctor?' said Marie, her apron at her mouth.

'No,' I protested.

'The fire's gone out,' said Marie helpfully. 'I'll light it.' And she reached for the tinderbox on the table. Never have I moved more quickly. Another gobbet of blood filled my mouth and ran violently down my nose.

'Thank you,' I said, firmly taking the tinderbox from her hand. 'A bowl of water is all I need, and some peace.'

Marie looked injured by my outburst, but did as she was bid. Hastily, I dressed.

When she returned she said, 'Last night there was another of those wolf attacks, and this time the beast came into the heart of the town.'

'Who was killed?' I asked as I washed my face.

She named a man I had not known.

'We will be next if that nosebleed of yours does not stop. I am told that wolves can smell blood from as far away as . . .' Here Marie paused to think. 'As far away as Spain,' she said with pride, as if at last she had pin-pointed the cause of all our troubles.

'Was the man torn to death?' I asked.

'No,' said Marie, disappointed that she had to tell the truth for the story did not quite have the dramatic ring to it that she would have liked.

'He left the tavern last night and was returning home when he saw a wolf, larger than any wolf seen before by man.'

My nose ached with bleeding. I waited to be told that what was left of him lay in a pool of blood.

'They say he had been gone from the tavern less than five minutes when he came back, belly churned and white with fear. He dropped dead of fright, he did, then and there. Dead as a door knocker. But before he died he said he had seen a wolf walking like a man on its hind legs, as tall as the houses themselves.' Her voice fell to a whisper. 'In its arms it carried a sleeping maiden.'

I was more shocked by this revelation than Marie could know.

I put on my cloak and hat, and made sure that the tinderbox was safe inside my doublet.

Marie said, 'I would not go out, sir. Not with your nose on the brink.'

'Thank you, Marie,' I said and made to leave. 'A wolf will take a while to arrive here from Spain.'

I, who had so long wondered if all this was a dream, had proof that Safire had indeed been brought to me, carried by the wolf from the chamber of gold. I was alive, not a ghost with whom Death was playing. I was alive, and my dream of marrying Safire belonged to the land of waking, not to the land of the dead.

Outside the air was cold and clammy. I decided that

come the night I would take Safire
away from here. So lost in thought
was I that I hardly knew where I was
going. Then I glimpsed a flash of red and
my guts turned to water. Why then did I
follow her? To ask her to forgive me, to stop
haunting me? I stayed several paces behind her as
down towards the river we went. Here the sky was
hung with dirty sheets put out to dry, their folds filled
with snow. The river lapped sluggishly at the shoreline
and a mist sat heavy upon it. She stopped by the water's
edge and watched the bargemen unloading their boats.

    'I'm sorry,' I said to her.

    She walked away from the river in the direction of the
tavern and I thought she had vanished in the mist when I
heard a sound, a low growl. The bargemen stopped what they
were doing and their backs straightened as they turned in my
direction. That was when I saw the huge hound. Between its
teeth it held a rag doll.

    I was nearly upon the animal when the doll dropped
from the creature's jaws. The girl had bent down, her red cloak
spread upon the ground, her face hidden in its hood. Slowly
she lifted her head. Her flesh had gone to bone, her dead eyes
stared straight into me. I glanced at the bargemen as they came
running and when I looked back the girl had disappeared and
it was no doll that lay broken upon the ground, but a dead
child.

The bargemen took hold of me.

'It is you,' they shouted together. 'We saw you.'

As a crowd gathered round us, the bargemen cried, 'We have caught him – we have caught the wolf man.'

Chapter Twenty-Eight

The news that the devil had been caught by the river spread through the town like piss against a wall running into the gutter. Out of every nook and cranny they came, gathering in number. Down from the market square, out of the tumbled houses spilled the entrails of the ravenous crowd. They had come to ogle the corpse, and me – the wolf man.

I was saved – if saved I was – by the bailiff and his soldiers who plucked me from the claws of the crowd and bundled me into a cart. It was driven fast over unforgiving cobbles, up twisting lanes where the shutters chattered and the crooked wooden beams of the buildings rattled with the tales of my crimes. A kite tail of the crowd ran behind, shouting.

'Here is the wolf man!'

'We have the wolf man!'

All the while I believed that I still had the tinderbox.

But when I felt my pocket there was nothing there. Time stopped. Everything faded away. Could it have fallen out in the skirmish? No, it wasn't possible. I remember feeling it and I had minded nothing else but not to have it torn from me. I am told a desert is full of endless sand. If my soul was filled with anything then it was dust and the ashes of possibilities. Suddenly I cared little what happened. So much more was lost than just the tinderbox. Safire, I had lost Safire. What now, I asked myself, what now?

The prison was in a round tower attached to the duke's castle. Behind a desk sat the Clerk to the Court. He meticulously wrote down all the garments as the soldiers stripped them from me.

Item: Hat, battered.

Item: Cloak, torn.

Item: Ruff, soiled.

Item: Doublet, mud-stained.

They stopped at breeches, shirt and boots for I refused to take them off and such was my rage that both he and the bailiff thought better than to try.

My cell was at the top of the tower. At least I had a good view from my two small slits of windows. I could see in the distance, over the chimney stacks, the castle where Safire was held. Below me in the market square a crowd had gathered, its hum a nest of wasps, their voices rising higher until one of the many nameless took it upon himself to read out the list of my supposed victims. The survivors, for there were a few, were

222

brought out like trophies to bear witness to my guilt. They were agreed on one thing: that the devil had come to earth in the shape of a wolf. It was this wolf who had caused the failing harvest, who was responsible for the taxes rising, who had made the forest unsafe.

I sat on the stinking straw resigned to my fate. If only I hadn't followed her, the girl with the red cloak. I put my head back, felt the cold of the stone. I had always told myself that I would rather go into battle than think of her again. I dared myself to remember what I would have given the world to forget.

It had happened after the soldiers had caught me, after my family had been murdered. They were stinking drunk. Always drunk. They dragged me at first by a rope as if I was an animal, told me in detail what they would do to me if I did not join them.

Next day we came across another farm just like our farm. The farmer greeted us, offered all he had in the hope that we would leave peacefully. The girl was thirteen winters old. She wore a red cape with the hood up to hide her face. She brought us the food, fresh-risen bread and homemade beer. We sat in the sunshine and the soldiers leered at her, and poured drink down my throat until farm, sky, fields, tipped upside down.

It happened so fast, the killing of that farmer and his wife. The girl in the red cloak tried to run. The soldiers caught her and brought her back to me, pulled down my breeches, told me to prove myself a man. I wouldn't. I couldn't. I threw up.

224

I think it was then that I became old before my tomorrows. All that was pure in me lost, all belief washed from me.

'Then let us show you how it should be done.'

They seized the terrified girl, pushed her hood off her face and threw her to the ground. One of the soldiers pulled up her skirts. I still can hear her scream. I picked up a pistol and pulled the trigger before anyone could take away her innocence, do to her what had been done to my sister. I shot her in the heart. I remember the look in her eyes in the moment of her dying. You never forget the first person you kill. Her soul has haunted me ever since. Last night I thought I was free. Perhaps I never will be.

Chapter Twenty-Nine

My trial was a farce. I had been assigned a lawyer, a thin quill of a man without a point. He refused to come into my prison cell, preferring instead to talk to me through the iron bars.

His advice, for what it was worth, was that I should confess to my crimes if I did not want to be questioned under torture, which he informed me was most distressing to watch.

I decided then and there that I would give no one the pleasure of seeing my knees shake or my voice tremble with fear. I would be bold for boldness had brought me Safire and it was with boldness I would go to the gallows.

'Your job is to make sure that doesn't happen,' I said.

'The court,' he mumbled, 'wants a full confession. It cannot hang you without one.'

'That is most reassuring.'

'I think I should tell you that the hangman is fond of his fiddlestick,' said my quill of a lawyer.

'A musician, is he?' I asked.

He said no more but disappeared into the gloom and all that could be heard of him were his heels on the stone.

'Useless numbskull!' I shouted after him.

Late that evening, I was dragged through endless passageways to the torture chamber.

By tomorrow night,' said the bailiff, 'we will have had a hanging and wedding.'

I was so enraged at the pig stupidity of the town that I fought as hard as the chains would allow until I was hauled down an eternity of stairs, deep into the cellars.

Here a wooden door led into a chamber that had never seen the light of day, its arched brick ceiling spoke of twisted spines. Its furnishings brought no comfort; a rack, chains and various other instruments of torture were laid out ready for use. The place sickened my soul for the walls still held the cries of yesterday's condemned, and the smell of burned flesh lingered.

The hangman stood waiting in the shadow, clicking his knuckles, his face lit by the glow from an iron stove. He looked neither pleased nor worried by the task ahead of him. More, I thought, his face showed indifference.

At a long bench sat the bailiff, the judge, a clerk, a scribe, a doctor and two master burghers of the town as well as my quill of a pointless lawyer. His first encouraging question was to ask the bailiff if my bindings would hold. Oh, what I would have given at that moment still to have had the tinderbox.

My lawyer, as I expected, soon argued himself into a legal quagmire while the judge's stomach seemed to have more to say on the proceedings than the judge himself for it rumbled loudly, impatient either for its supper or the chamber pot. It struck me that it mattered little what anyone said as long as I confessed and did so relatively soon.

Finally, the judge, having had enough of my lawyer's ramblings, puffed himself up and said, 'Do you, Otto Hundebiss, plead guilty to the charge of wolfism?'

'No,' I said.

'Then you will be questioned under torture,' replied the judge.

'But your honour,' said my pointless quill of a lawyer, 'I have not yet finished.'

'Sir,' said the judge, 'we have waited all night for you to begin, let alone finish.'

As if mortally wounded by the remark my lawyer sank back into his seat.

The hangman stepped into the light. I could tell he had seen too much of death and dying to let torture bother him and doubted much if there would be any mercy in his treatment of me. The only defence I had was the truth, for that alone was baffling enough.

'Wait,' I said. 'I do confess to having power over three mighty wolves.'

There was silence. The judge thought about what I had said and waved the hangman back into the shadows.

The court clerk started to write furiously.

The judge said, 'Do you confess to the crime of wolfism, of eating of human flesh?'

'No, your honour, I do not. I have never been a werewolf.'

'Are you confessing, sir, or are you wasting the court's time? Hangman!' shouted the judge.

The hangman sprang forward.

'Wait, wait,' I said. 'The wolves of which I speak indeed have supernatural powers but they are to be thanked, not blamed.'

'What?' said the judge. 'Thanked?'

'Yes, sir. For they alone have saved this dukedom from the devastation of war, kept away marauding soldiers and highwaymen, made it safe for the crops to be planted, to be harvested. They have never hurt anyone who lives here in this town. And what is more, you all know this to be the truth.'

The judge looked up from his papers.

'Unless you confess to being the werewolf, you will be questioned under torture. Do I make myself clear? Hangman, begin.'

'Don't you see? Someone in your town is responsible for these killings. These crimes of which I am accused were not committed by any werewolf but by men with the help of ravaging hounds.'

'Quiet, sir!' shouted the judge.

At that moment a young servant entered the chamber and handed the now scarlet-faced judge a note. The judge read it, furiously screwed it up and, throwing it across the stone floor, let out a loud fart.

'Hangman, begin,' he repeated.

My clothes were stripped from me and I stood stark naked in front of the court until a loincloth was put round me. Then my wrists were tied fast to the chains hanging from the ceiling and I was winched up until my feet left the ground, they too being tied down so I was spread-eagled like a lump of meat on a butcher's hook.

With dread I watched as the hangman brought from the stove a burning rod that glowed white hot. I braced myself. My eyes closed, I felt the heat of the rod as it came closer.

'I call this my fiddlestick,' said the hangman. 'Shall we see what music you can make?'

The sound of chairs being scraped back made me open my eyes. The judge and the court officials were standing and bowing. A grandly dressed man wearing chains of office had entered the chamber. His hair was thick and white, though he was ghost-thin. I thought he was old but in the dim light I could not be sure. With him came four soldiers dressed in black.

'Your Grace,' said the judge, 'we are about to extract a confession.'

The ghost of a man said, 'That I can see well enough. Hangman, step away.'

The fiddlestick re-entered the fire.

'Be gone, all of you,' said the ghost of a man. 'I wish to speak alone with the prisoner.'

'But sir,' said the judge, 'this is . . . '

The soldiers stepped forward and the judge, seeing that his authority had no more value, retired, or rather his portly stomach retired and he followed, as did the rest of the court officials. One of the soldiers cut me down and I was ordered to dress. Then stumbling, I was taken to the bench where the ghost of a man sat. For the first time I could see him clearly and wondered if my eyes deceived me, for it looked as if his face and body were covered with tiny silver spiders, spinning frozen cobwebs all over him. As I watched, their delicate design stitched him to his chair.

I blinked and looked again. What I saw was a man who appeared ill, the very sap of him being drained away by those spinning spiders.

He perused the judge's notes.

'Dog bite, that is what your name means,' he said at last, his words expressionless.

'Yes, Your Grace,' I said.

He swept his hand over the bench and sent the papers flying.

'Who are you?' he asked.

I knew by the manner in which the judge had addressed him that this was the duke, Safire's father, and it would be best if I told the truth. Nearly all the truth, but not quite, for

I would not tell him that the three wolves were his sons. That information I had decided to bury deep in my heart. Anyway, what did it matter? I no longer had the tinderbox.

'I was a soldier, sir.'

'Where are you from?'

'The lowlands. I am a farmer's boy, drummed into fight when I was fourteen after my family was murdered.'

'How old are you now?'

'Eighteen, sir.'

'How is it that you are here in this town?'

'I was fighting at Breitenfeld when I was wounded. I found myself in a forest and once I had regained my strength I came here by chance.'

'You are charged with the crime of wolfism.'

'I am no werewolf, sir, though for a short time I had the power to call forth wolves.'

'Then do so now,' commanded the ghost of a man. 'Let me see for myself.'

'I cannot, sir. I no longer have the power. It was but lent to me.'

He sniffed.

'Where did you find this so-called power?'

'In a castle built between three mighty oak trees in the forest.'

He looked at me, his eyes almost as white as his skin and I saw that he was nowhere near as old as the silver spiders made him appear.

'You have been there and you survived?' he asked.

'Yes, sir. Up to now that is.'

'Tell me about the mistress of the castle. Did you see her?'

'I called her the Lady of the Nail on account of her thumbnail. It was long and curled round and round.'

'The Lady of the Nail,' he repeated. 'Most apt. There are reports that she is dead.'

'She is, sir.'

'How did she die?'

'She was killed by the wolves and her castle tumbled down. Where it fell fire sprang up and from the fire saplings grew.'

'She is dead – you are sure of that?'

'I saw the remains of her lying in an ocean of blood.'

The ghost of a man was silent for a long time, so long that the walls began to whisper.

'What do you see when you look at me?' he asked at last.

'Spiders, sir, that are making small silvery cobwebs over all of you.'

'If the lady was dead, I would be well again and I am not.'

I had nothing to fear by telling him the truth. The gallows were waiting for me.

'It's the duchess's doing.'

'What do you mean?'

I went closer to him. The soldiers moved towards me but the cobwebbed duke waved his hand and they once more stood silent against the wall.

'Tell me what you know,' he said.

I told him what I had overheard in the domed room, that the wife of the duke shared her bed with the prince, and as I spoke the spiders span busily around his head as if to muffle my voice. Pull as he might at the thin cobwebs, still those spiders span.

'Tell me . . . tell me more.'

His speech was limping now.

I said I had heard that if the Lady Safire was to marry anyone other than the prince, the duchess and her lover would die.

'If anyone should stand trial today it is the duchess for the spell she has cast on you.'

For a while he said nothing, his face blank, white, dead white.

'My life . . . is little more than sleep,' he said at last. 'A living death that robs me of my days . . . I cannot remember why I am here. Safire pleaded with me . . . '

'Please, Your Grace,' I said, 'I have not one drop of noble blood in me with which to claim your daughter but I would be true to her to the day I died.'

He stared up at me with the saddest of eyes.

'Tomorrow you will be hanged . . . and my daughter will marry the prince.'

'If I am to hang then let me be hanged for loving your daughter and for no other crime.'

Wearily he stood up, shaking his head.

236

'Tinder . . . the sweetest child of my heart . . . '

He left, trailing a cloak of cobwebs behind him.

In that moment as the court officials returned, I took my chance. I pulled the fiddlestick from the stove and using it as a sword, rushed first at the bailiff. He screamed as the fiddlestick caught the side of his face. I had reached the stairs when the hangman came for me, and everything went black.

Chapter Thirty

All around me stand the heedless and headless dressed in their finest clothes. White lace ruffs frame the faces of a fox, a magpie, a badger, a crow, all the creatures of the forest greeting and meeting one another as if such conversations with ravens were commonplace.

Broken citizens of this town. Dancing ladies. Roaring boys. Forsaken gentlemen. Each of their heads exchanged for the beast and the wing.

Beside me stands the Lady of the Nail.

'What do you think to my fraternity of macemongers?'

'Who are they?' I ask.

She laughs.

'It is enough to know, too much to see,' she says.
'Why, here is my sister, Mistress Jabber.'
She points her long nail to a fine lady dressed in
velvet and brocade, jewels shimmer on her gloved
hand. She has the head of a magpie.
'The prince?' I ask.
'Why, the fox, of course,' says the Lady of the Nail.
'Who else could he be?'
The fox looks vicious, cruel.
Could not he kill the magpie?'
'Shall I tell you a secret? He would if he could. But
the magpie would pluck his eyes out for gems well
before he could sink his teeth into her feathery flesh.'
'The duke – which one of these animals is the duke?'
'There,' she says. 'The poor soul with the badger's
head, buried in his sett of dreams.'
'Safire? Where is Safire?' I feel panic rising.
'What have you done with her?'
'It is enough to know, too much to see,'
says the Lady of the Nail.
I am shouting as she vanishes along with her guests.
And standing not far away is my Safire. She is
imprisoned in her clothes by criss-crossed ribbons
of armour, her head served on a plate of the finest
starched lace. She wears embroidered gloves and my
ring no longer fits her finger but sits at the tip, as if

at any moment it will fall off. I go to her and with
every step she is farther away.
'What do the dice tell you?' she calls.
I am surprised to find I am holding them
in my hand. I throw them down.
'Four jacks and a nine,' I tell her.
'Which direction?'
I cannot remember what the nine stands for, what
the half-beast half-man said.
'I don't know,' I say.
She opens her hands and in them is a small flame.
It flickers as if it could take flight. She throws the orb
of burning gold and it comes towards me, growing
in size until all is lost in white light.

'Wake up,' shouted the bailiff, pulling me to my feet. The room swam before me, the light too bright, my head full to bursting with molten lead.

'We wouldn't want you to miss your own death,' said the bailiff. 'Come on, wake up.'

All I wanted was quiet, to close my eyes again, to be able to return to where I would see my Safire, for it worried me that I couldn't remember if my ring fell from her finger.

'Wake up, I say,' shouted the bailiff. 'You will have an eternity in hell in which to dream. Look, it is a beautiful day for

a hanging and an even better day for
a wedding.'

The hangman, dressed in a smart
doublet and breeches of leather, came into
the cell accompanied by a dough-faced priest, all
shaky and risen with fear.

The hangman studied me with a look of regret.

'Usually,' he said, 'I shave your head but there being a
wedding, time is short. Especially as I want your hanging to be
slow and painful. You will have to go to the gallows as you stand.'

'Am I not a lucky dog?' I said.

He huffed and jutted his jaw so that the few remaining brown teeth could be seen.

'You will twist on that rope until you wish you were dead. How much do you weigh?'

'I don't know,' I replied.

'How tall?'

'What does all this matter?'

'Because I don't want the rope to snap when I kick away the ladder,' said the hangman.

'Has that ever happened?' I asked.

'Never. And it never will. Not on my watch,' he said, sucking on the remains of his teeth as he made his calculations. 'Priest, we should get started.'

The priest went ash-white and promptly fainted away.

'No breakfast,' said the bailiff and, cursing under his breath, carried him out, narrowly avoiding a collision with my quill of a lawyer.

'I am in demand this morning,' I said with as much cheer as I could muster.

'I would like a word with the prisoner,' said the lawyer to the hangman and the bailiff. 'In private, if you don't mind.'

Both men went reluctantly. They hovered by the cell door, ears flapping.

The lawyer who only yesterday had been too frightened to come near me had overnight been miraculously cured.

He came as close as he dared, which was very close, and said in a legal, hushed tone that only I could hear, 'If you were to tell His Highness the prince where the tinderbox was hidden, things may go better for you.'

'How much better?'

'He might consider a reprieve.'

'That's in the duke's power to grant, not the prince's.'

The lawyer cleared his throat.

Now at last I saw the point to my quill of a lawyer and burst out laughing.

'Tell me, where does the sun rise?'

He looked taken aback by the question and, judging my mind unhinged by the prospect of my imminent death, said indulgently, 'In the east.'

'Quite. And I would be a fool, wouldn't I, if I believed it rose in the west?'

'Yes.'

'And a bigger fool still to believe there would be a reprieve, even if I knew what you were talking about?'

'Just tell me where it is, that is all,' insisted the quill of a lawyer.

'Surely,' I said, 'such a wealthy man as the prince has many tinderboxes in his household. Why would I know where he keeps them all? I am no cunning man.'

This conversation was giving me time to try and wriggle my fingers free in the hope of loosening the rope that bound my hands.

The lawyer's lips pursed tight in his face as if his features were too bitter to bear.

'I believe that you know exactly what the prince is talking about.'

I decided to remain mute, as I had, by then, loosened the ropes considerably.

'All I can say,' he spat in my face, 'is that I hope you burn in hell.'

He stomped away.

The executioner's procession was a grander affair than I had imagined such a town putting on. I was surrounded by the duke's soldiers. Before me was the bailiff, the judge, the court clerks, the priest, the doctor and other notables. Behind me, dressed in all his finery, walked the hangman. I reckoned it would not now take much to free my hands, so I held the rope tight to make it look as if I was still bound. The hangman was followed by the good burghers of the town, all of them fattened off the cattle market of the poor, all of them hungry for a slaughter, for a veil to be drawn over the wolf murders.

It was then I remembered that in my dream I had rolled four Jacks and a nine. I knew now what the nine meant. Somehow that knowledge cheered me, for the notion that death has a direction to it amused me. I was, by the wisdom of red dots on white ivory, to travel back to where I had come from and I was somewhat pleased to note that the half-beast half-man's dice had such wit to them, for by his direction I would have travelled full circle.

As we entered the market square a huge cheer went up. One lad could be heard above the noise, singing in a voice only given to angels.

'Even a man who's pure in heart
and says his prayers by night
may become a wolf
when the wolfsbane blooms
and the autumn moon is bright.'

'Hang him,' cried the crowd. 'Put him on the wheel! Death is too good for the likes of him.'

This was greeted with much hooping and whooping. It was clear the celebration had already begun.

Chapter Thirty-One

It seemed to me that the whole town had gathered in the market square. Many were garishly dressed. They had a grim determination to be merry and flags flew from houses in the crisp air. On the platform sat the master burghers, the town councillors and the judge, waiting for the arrival of the duke's party. Even though times were hard, this would be a day to remember, one to tell your grandchildren of, when the town had finally rid itself of the werewolf, the day the duke's daughter had been set free to marry.

A trumpet sounded and everybody was still. Those on the platform stood to attention as two carriages drew up and the crowd separated to make way for the duke's entourage. Slowly from one carriage stepped the duke, his cobweb cloak trailing behind him. A gasp rippled around the crowd. The duchess walked beside him, resplendent in a dress cut low and sprinkled with jewels. She held in her gloved hand the edge of the cobweb cloak, her irritation with her husband was palpable as he mounted the steps to the platform and painfully took his seat.

Next to arrive was the prince. He looked impatient for this to be over. Who could blame him? He sat on the other side of the duke.

The church bells rang and, without asking the duke, the prince nodded to the judge, who stood and read my sentence.

I was relieved that my Safire was not there to witness my end, better by far that she believed me to belong to a land of dreams, for I would never wish to haunt her, as those I have killed, and seen killed, have haunted me.

The drums began to roll. Death had finally hunted me down. With one practised movement the hangman had me up the ladder and the noose secured round my neck.

The crowd fell silent, for it was the custom that the condemned man should speak his last words to the onlookers. I didn't ask for mercy for I knew there was none. I wished I could ask for my tinderbox.

'Hang him, hang him slow,' shouted the crowd. 'Hang him good and proper.'

With my loosened hand, I tried to fight the hangman. This was my last living chance. Laughing, he kicked away the ladder.

I am on a road walking home from war when I see a tree. The trunk is made from the bodies of dead soldiers, the branches are the soldiers' arms and hands. By the grass verge stands an old witch.
'Who are you?' I ask.
'The witch who waits for the soldier returning home from war.'
'Why do you wait?'
'For my tinderbox to be returned to me.'
'What is down the tree?'
'The dogs of war.'

Chapter Thirty-Two

The ladder disappeared from beneath me and the earth called my body to the grave. With a jolt my legs found they were kicking at the space between the sky and the straw. I heard the rushing of my life as it went past me, my eyes bulged from my skull, all breath sucked out of me. I was lost in gluey darkness.

Something snapped. It was over. My end was as sudden as my beginning. I fell hard on a sharp object that sent a strike of pain through me, kept my senses there. I was on the straw at the bottom of the scaffold, blue sky above me. I pulled frantically at the ropes binding my hands. Finally free of them, I tore the noose from round my neck and took in deep, glorious gulps of air. And in that moment before life found the right beat on which to restart, I knew I'd landed on a familiar object. I struck steel against flint once, then twice, then three times.

I heard a terrified gasp. It rose as a wind from the crowd.

I found my feet, saw the petrified faces of the judge, the bailiff and the hangman. Standing on the platform were not the three men from the chambers of bronze, silver and gold, but the three mighty wolves, each more ominous than the other. So massive was the wolf from the chamber of gold that he towered above the houses, above the town wall, near high as the church steeple. Now I heard the silence, for the silence of fear is three times louder than any other silence. It was broken by the prince, who threw himself upon the ground, as did the duchess. She crawled towards her lover, one of her breasts coming free from her gown.

So great was this wolf that the platform broke beneath his weight and the councillors, the master burghers, the prince, the duchess crumpled into the crack at his paw. All, now careless of rank and order, scrambled to safety or slid unceremoniously off the platform. The crowd began to rush and whirl as does water brought to the boil.

Only the duke stood tall in his cobweb cloak amid the sea of abandoned hats and swords. Papers took flight over the market square, the sky darkened and snow began to fall in huge flakes.

The wolf from the chamber of silver pulled up the gallows, crushing it in his paws, as if it was nothing more than balsa wood.

'Master, what is it that you desire?' The wolf from the chamber of bronze growled over the crowd, who stopped and turned.

'Bring me those who committed the crimes for which I was to be hanged,' I cried.

The wolf disappeared and in less than a strike from the town hall clock reappeared with the coffin-maker and his ravenous hounds.

'No,' screamed the coffin-maker, 'I'm innocent. These are the prince's hounds.'

No one moved.

The wolf from the chamber of bronze pushed the duchess and the prince back to the broken platform.

'They paid the coffin-maker to buy the hounds that murdered the good citizens of this town,' said the wolf from the chamber of bronze.

At that moment, voices rose and the news rushed to us that an army was coming.

'If you harm me you will all suffer,' shouted the prince, 'for my army will take no prisoners.'

The wolf from the chamber of silver stepped forward.

'Master, what is it that you desire?' His voice shook the window panes.

'That the army be vanquished and the prince be punished for his crimes as you see fit,' I said.

No sooner had the words left my mouth than the wolf from the chamber of silver grabbed hold of the prince and, before the man knew what was happening, there was a mighty roar like thunder and at the speed of a lightning strike the prince was devoured. All that was left of him was blood and guts which slipped onto the snow.

'No,' screamed the duchess. 'No!'

Her words were lost in a low snarl as the wolf returned. In his mighty jaws he held the banners of the prince's army.

The bailiff looked at the duke, who had regained some of his colour.

'Arrest the coffin-maker – and that woman,' ordered the duke, pointing to the duchess. 'Take the hounds away and destroy them.'

'Don't touch me,' shouted the duchess on shaking legs, as soldiers dragged her and the coffin-maker away.

Now the wolf from the chamber of gold stepped forward.

'Master, what is it that you desire?'

Before I could answer Safire ran into the square, her hair fire-wild about her, her wedding dress hitched up and boy's boots on her feet. Ready for battle, she wielded a rapier.

'Do not lay a hand on him, do not lay a finger on my Otto, my love,' she shouted. 'I will kill anyone who hurts him.'

I jumped from the broken platform and the crowd parted to let me through. Safire and I collided as I imagine comets do when blazing through the sky. I lifted her off her feet and whirled her round. As we spun – once, twice, thrice – the wolves disappeared.

Chapter Thirty-Three

We are married. All that I had ever desired has come true, and more.

Almost as soon as the duke gave us his blessing he began to recover his strength and now the cobwebs have vanished and the father that Safire had lost has returned. It was a strange thing, for after the wolves had gone I wasn't certain if the townsfolk would turn on me, but it was as if they had forgotten all that they had seen, only witnessed and remembered who the true villains were. Justice was done that day. The coffin-maker was hanged on a rope that did not break. There was no need to execute the duchess. Her death was assured by our marriage. In that the Lady of the Nail has kept her word.

Now it is night. The snow has brought a silence to the town, whitened the roofs, illuminated the sky. The feasting is over and Safire will come to me as my wife. My head swims

with a happiness that I have never known. To find some
sobriety, I decide to take the night air. Only the tinderbox
worries at me, for I no longer want it. The battlements look
on to the river and in that crisp night air I stare into the icy
waters and up at the moon.

'Oh, thank you for this,' I say to no one.

'Otto,' says a voice behind me. I turn and I cannot see
him for he is hidden in the shadows.

'Show yourself,' I say.

'I want my dice back.'

'Where are you?'

'Do you still have them?'

'Yes. You can have them back. I don't need them
anymore, I'm where I should be.'

'What did they tell you, Otto, when you last threw
them down?'

'Four Jacks and a nine. West. But they were wrong.'

I take the cloth bag from my pocket and throw it
down as bait to draw him out.

'What will you do with the tinderbox?'

'What I want to do, I cannot. I want to free Safire's
brothers.'

There is silence and I wonder if I am talking to
myself.

I jump when I hear him not far from me.

'Only one of their flesh has the power to free them.'

'What if I give the tinderbox to Safire to strike?'

262

'Then you will find yourself where I first found you, wounded in the forest, before all this enchantment happened. Death will be waiting for you. Perhaps you can cheat him, perhaps not. I cannot tell you which direction the road will take you. All I know is that your boots belong on my pole. And the dice are mine.'

'Wait,' I shout. 'You said when I fell in love I would come into my kingdom – and I have.'

'Is everything all right, sir?' says the night watchman.

'Yes, yes,' I say and wait until the watchman is gone. I search the shadows but the half-beast half-man has vanished and so have his dice.

Shaken, I take from inside my doublet the tinderbox. Rocks did not shatter it, fire did not destroy it, burying did not hide it. Perhaps water will drown it. I throw it down, it falls and hits the ice, bursting into flames before it melts away.

'What's happening?' shout the soldiers.

'All is well,' I say. And I know all is well. I have freed myself of a terrible weight. I would not be lying to Safire if I said I could not free her brothers, it would be the truth. I fair dance down the steps. Servants bow to me, I am lord and master and my soul is at peace. The chamber is lit with dozens of candles, the tapestries and drapes are the finest and there stands our wedding bed, waiting for us. My life has just begun.

Safire is naked beneath her muslin gown.

'Otto,' she says, 'how well you understand me. This is the most perfect wedding gift.'

She shows me what she is holding.

It is here. The tinderbox. Washed clean, lacquered black, her name on it in gold spindly writing.

At that moment a gust of wind blows out all the candles.

'Let me light them,' she says.

Words are frozen in me. The steel strikes the flint. The spark flies.

I am in the midst of the battle, trapped in the great forest, caught between the criss-cross of trees. About me lay the dead and the dying, their blood – our blood – made the carpet of leaves more crimson than autumn had intended.

That is when I see Death.

Author's Note

I have long been fascinated by *The Tinderbox*, the first story Hans Christian Andersen wrote. He was twenty-nine when it was published in May 1835 and embarrassingly short of money. Andersen took inspiration for *The Tinderbox* from a much-loved folk tale of his childhood, *The Spirit in the Candle*. I wanted to find a way to retell the story in a historical context but with a modern resonance.

I was inspired by a conversation. I met a soldier who had served in Iraq and who felt that war had left him with little except nightmares. He was not the only serving officer I spoke to. I heard first-hand stories from soldiers who had returned from Afghanistan and were trying to deal with the echoes of war. All these young men found it hard to adjust to civilian life. 'It seems so dead,' one told me. 'You only know you are alive when you dance on the edge.'

My research led me to look at the experiences of the boy soldiers of Rwanda, at the horrific tales of rape and slaughter. How do you grow up and live a normal life when you have seen so much death? Battles, whether fought with machetes or machine-guns, swords or muskets, have had the same effect throughout history: the devastation of the lives of men, women and children.

I chose to place my story at the time of the Thirty Years War (1618-1648) and for this, and for his patience with me - a story-teller, not a historian - I must thank Peter H Wilson, author of *The Thirty Years War: Europe's Tragedy*. A meeting with him convinced me that this much-neglected part of European history was the right setting for *Tinder*. It was a war in which most European countries played a role, a war that destroyed Germany, nibbling at its borders and sowing the seeds of the First and Second World Wars.

A fairy tale is a fascinating medium in which to examine conflict, love and loss - for all good fairy stories have dark and light at their heart. This is my retelling of *The Tinderbox*, and it is with the greatest admiration for Hans Christian Andersen, the master of the fairy tale, that I have told my story.

Sally Gardner

Acknowledgments

As a young adult I was heartbroken that being
grown-up meant reading books without illustrations
and I had a vision that this story would be
illustrated. David Roberts put his soul into the
drawings for *Tinder*, for which he has my deepest
gratitude. I want to thank Sue Michniewicz who
worked tirelessly with David on the inside design,
and Laura Brett who helped to design the jacket.

I would also like to thank my personal editor,
Jacky Bateman, for making me laugh on my darkest
days, and my editor at Orion, Fiona Kennedy for
her constant support.

Sally Gardner
London
August 2013

OTHER TITLES FOR OLDER READERS
BY SALLY GARDNER

I, Coriander
The Red Necklace
The Silver Blade
The Double Shadow

First published in Great Britain in 2013
by Indigo
This paperback edition first published in Great Britain in 2015
by Indigo
An imprint of Hachette Children's Group
Part of Hodder & Stoughton
Carmelite House
50 Victoria Embankment
London EC4Y 0DZ
An Hachette UK Company

Text © Sally Gardner 2013
Illustrations ©David Roberts 2013

A CIP catalogue record for this book is available from the British Library.

ISBN 978 1 78062 148 7

2 4 6 8 10 9 7 5 3 1

Printed in China

www.orionchildrensbooks.com

MIX
Paper from
responsible sources
FSC® C104740
FSC
www.fsc.org